MW00618066

DX Brings Danger
By Walker A. Tompkins

mys
F TOM

Other Tommy Rockford adventures

SOS at Midnight
CQ Ghost Ship !
Death Valley QTH

$5.—

*For James Norris
and the fine
folks at KBLS*

900968

CONTENTS

DX Brings Danger

CHAPTER ONE

INVITATION TO ADVENTURE

T he mysterious telegram had been delayed twenty-four hours
before it was finally delivered to Tommy Rockford in the beach
cottage in Washington State where he was vacationing with
Uncle JC. Its arrival interrupted his packing for a mountain-climbing
trip to Mt. Rainier National Park next day.

The delay in transit was explained by a note scrawled on the yellow
envelope: *Missent to Ocean Park Calif.* Since the wire came from Santa
Bonita, his home town in Southern California, Tommy assumed it
was from his parents. They always worried when he was away scaling
cliffs and glaciers.

But it was from a schoolfriend, not his folks:

TOMMY ROCKFORD
c/o J C ELLISON
OCEAN PARK WASHINGTON
  TELEPHONE ME IMMEDIATELY
  REPEAT IMMEDIATELY STOP
  HAVE URGENT NEWS UTMOST IMPORTANCE STOP
  73 SPUD WA6IBR

Tommy's blue eyes twinkled with amusement. Spud Kleveland
was a bookish fifteen-year-old sophomore who was breaking in this
summer as a cub reporter on his father's daily newspaper, the Santa
Bonita *News-Star*. He always took himself very seriously.

Tommy had coached Spud in radio theory and Morse code last

winter, enabling Spud to get on the air as the operator of amateur radio station WA6IBR. The cryptic symbol 73 that ended Spud's telegram meant "best regards" in radio slang.

"Now why," wondered Tommy, "would Spud ask me to waste perfectly good money calling him long distance—when he knows we have a ham radio schedule tonight on twenty meters?"

Tommy's ham radio call sign was K6ATX.

He glanced at his new wristwatch—one of the solar-powered models, which his parents had given him as a high school graduation gift six weeks before—and saw that it was seven o'clock, just one hour away from his regular Saturday night radio appointment with Spud.

Ham radio was a lot easier mode of communication than writing letters. And thanks to a telephone patch that linked Spud's radio station with Tommy's home telephone, he could keep in close touch with his parents as well.

"Might as well keep on packing," Tommy decided. "One more hour's wait won't hurt, and I can save myself a long-distance charge."

Or would it hurt? Spud had been most emphatic about the urgency of his "news of utmost importance," repeating the word "immediately." On the other hand, Tommy knew Spud was an excitable kid. A millionaire's son, he had no idea what telephone calls cost.

Tommy wished his uncle had been there to advise him, but J. C. Ellison was in Seattle, arranging to adopt a recently orphaned Ocean Park youth, "Noisy" Noyce, as his own son. The three of them had just emerged from a grueling adventure involving a mad scientist in a ghost ship, a few miles north of Ocean Park.*

Trying to put Spud's enigmatic message out of his mind, Tommy returned to the chore of packing his coils of nylon rope, pitons, ice ax, spiked boots and other mountaineering paraphernalia, taking them out to his car in preparation for a before-daylight start to Mt. Rainier in the morning.

Blond-headed Tommy had the rugged physique that high-altitude rock climbing demanded. A week away from his eighteenth birthday, Tommy Rockford stood an even six feet, and his 185 pounds of lean muscle attested to the fine conditioning he had received during the three seasons he had played varsity halfback at Santa Bonita High.

---

*See *CQ GHOST SHIP!* ARRL, 1985

Because of his outstanding athletic and scholastic record, Tommy had been approached by scouts from USC, Washington, UCLA, Stanford and other universities who offered him attractive scholarships to enroll in their schools. But much as he loved sports of all kinds, Tommy's only dream was to become an electronics engineer, specializing in the space-age science of telemetry.

The best school on the West Coast for that kind of training was the California Institute of Technology at Pasadena, where football was a gym course only. This was Tommy's last summer holiday before buckling down to the long, hard pull at Cal Tech that would lead to a degree in engineering.

At a quarter to eight Tommy left his packing and headed for the bedroom, where he had set up his summertime portable Amateur Radio station. It consisted of the bare essentials—a Heathkit HW-5400 transceiver, a battery-powered electronic Morse code keyer and a crystal mike.

The antenna for K6ATX here at the beach was a makeshift dipole strung between two pine trees. He had cut it for forty-meter work, but had been having excellent luck recently retuning the antenna and fishing for DX, or long-distance contacts, on twenty and ten meters.

Working Spud, a mere twelve hundred miles away, should be easy; several times during the past week Tommy had talked with hams in Europe, Asia and Australia, despite the low power of his equipment and the haywire antenna lash-up.

When he had switched on the rig, Tommy set the transceiver at exactly the same frequency on the twenty-meter phone band he and Spud used on their Saturday night ragchews, or QSOs, as hams called ed their two-way conversations. He was relieved to find that their chosen slot was relatively free tonight from QRM, or interfering signals.

At precisely eight o'clock Pacific Standard Time, Tommy pressed the "talk" button on his D104 microphone to put station K6ATX from receive to transmit. Then he began his routine calling sequence, well aware that unknown thousands of radio hams and SWLs, or short wave listeners, might be tuned to his voice all over the world:

"WA6IBR, WA6IBR, WA6IBR in Santa Bonita, California, here is K6ATX portable 7, K6ATX portable 7, K6ATX portable 7, calling on schedule and standing by. Copy, Spud?"

Three times Tommy repeated the sequence before releasing his thumb from the mike button, which automatically put K6ATX/7 back on receive. The usual QRN, or summer static, crackled so loudly from the speaker that Tommy switched to his rubber-cushioned headphones to reduce the unwanted noise.

He listened intently, tuning twenty kilohertz on either side of his calling frequency. If he got no answer inside of four minutes he would "QSY" to another prearranged frequency and try again on CW, or Continuous Wave Morse code—which was easier to punch through interference when conditions were rough.

But it was not necessary to QSY. He recognized Spud Kleveland's boyish treble coming back to his call: "K6ATX/7 in Ocean Park, Washington, here is WA6IBR in Santa Bonita California returning. Are we in business, Tommy? Over."

Even though Tommy's first QSO had been at the age of twelve, using a Novice Class license, he still got a thrill at completing a radio contact across hundreds of miles of distance.

"Copy you solid, Spud, five by seven signal, fine business."

A signal report of "five by seven" meant perfectly readable, moderately loud and clear reception. Since both boys worked "fast break-in," they did not have to sign their call with each transmission, a procedure that was legal as long as they identified their stations once every ten minutes.

"Tommy," Spud demanded in aggrieved tones, "why didn't you telephone me yesterday? Didn't you get my telegram? I've been on pins and needles for two days, waiting to hear from you!"

While Spud was talking, a ham in Wisconsin began exchanging weather reports with a KL7 somewhere in the State of Alaska, smack-dab on WA6IBR's frequency. Tommy switched on his audio notch filter and deftly nulled out the unwanted Wisconsin signal.

"Sorry, Spud," K6ATX came back, "but your QTC was mis-sent to Ocean Park *California* and I just got it an hour ago. Didn't see any sense wasting money on a land-line call. What's happening, man?"

There was a brief interval of QSB, or fading signals, but since Spud had the beginner's habit of repeating each sentence, Tommy did not miss the gist of his message:

"....ever since you saved my life from those kidnappers last winter, Dad's wanted to do you a favor in return, and now he has his chance. Can't tell you over the air, Tommy, with the whole world listening in. This deal is top secret, no kiddin'. So phone me collect right now, huh? Number's 686-3911. What I've got to tell you will skin the hair right off your head, pal. It will also bring you home as fast as your wheels will carry you."

Tommy said reluctantly, "Nothing could make me do that, kid, but QRX for a land-line call. K6ATX temporarily clear."

Tommy's fingers flew over the buttons on the telephone. When Spud answered—Tommy didn't have the gall to make it a collect call—Tommy said, "This had better be really good, man, seeing what this is costing me. Whoever heard of two radio hams resorting to the telephone?"

Spud came back with a gleeful chuckle. "You won't be sorry, pal. Listen: As soon as it gets dark Monday night, I'm taking off on a super-secret treasure hunting expedition to San Miguel Island with my father. You're the only outside guest invited to go along. So hop in that sports car of yours and burn the road south, Tommy. You can still make it in time if you start tonight."

Tommy scowled with annoyance. For as long as he could remember, people had been digging for treasure or Indian relics on San Miguel, an island located twenty-five miles off the coast of Southern California, the most westerly of the Channel Islands group. Spud's invitation did not interest him in the least.

"Sorry, but I have other plans, Spud," Tommy demurred. "The Los Padres Chapter of the Sierra Club is making a glacier climb at Mount Rainier this week and I'm going with them. Besides, Spud, San Miguel Island is a Navy bombing range. You couldn't land there anyway."

Spud made a long, gusty sigh into the telephone.

"My father has received a three-day clearance from the Navy to go ashore, Tommy. We can have from sunrise Tuesday through sunset Thursday before they start bombing practice again—three whole days."

"Still not interested," Tommy said grumpily.

"You will be when I tell you what we're going after...This is the secret I couldn't discuss over the air. Tommy, we know where to find the hulk of a phantom Spanish galleon that's been sunk off San Miguel Island since the year 1581 AD!"

Tommy said, "I've heard that story before, too. Sorry."

Spud went on talking as if he hadn't heard: "Dad has leased a remote-controlled submarine tractor, which carries an underwater television camera. After we locate the galleon on the TV screen, you can go down and explore it with your scuba diving outfit. There's something inside that phantom galleon that a diver can bring up. Something worth maybe half a million dollars in gold.

"Now are you coming down to join us, or not?"

CHAPTER TWO

AN ALARMING MYSTERY

In spite of his firm determination not to let anyone talk him out of his mountain-climbing trip, Tommy felt his pulses leap with excitement at Spud's invitation. Skin diving was a hobby that ranked equally with mountaineering in Tommy's versatile life—although ham radio was his all-time favorite hobby.

He forced himself to take a firm stand: "No-o, Spud, I'm sorry. Diving for a real Spanish galleon sounds mighty exciting, I'll admit, but I can't back out on my Sierra Club deal. Why don't you take along Doc Baldwin or Roy MacCormack? They're divers."

Spud Kleveland acted dumfounded at his friend's refusal.

"Aren't you even going to ask me what's *in* the galleon?"

"Okay, what's in the galleon—assuming there is a galleon?"

Spud inhaled a deep breath and began. "There's a chart nailed to the wall of the captain's cabin in the poop deck of that galleon that shows exactly where they buried Cabrillo four hundred and more years ago. And for the past forty or fifty years the governments of Spain and Portugal have posted a standing offer of half a million dollars for anyone who can locate Cabrillo's grave. You knew that, didn't you?"

Tommy wasn't too well versed on California's early history, having specialized in science all through high school, but every California schoolchild had been taught that a Portuguese navigator named Juan Rodriguez Cabrillo had discovered California in the year 1542, exactly fifty years after Columbus discovered the New World.

School children also knew that Cabrillo had died of blood poisoning while spending the winter of 1542-1543 on San Miguel Island, and had been buried in a grave that was lost to history.

All his life Tommy had heard of the big reward being offered to any scientific expedition that could return Cabrillo's skeleton in armor to his native land for enshrinement in a big cathedral. Many attempts had been made to find Cabrillo's grave, without success, and a few years back the US Navy had closed San Miguel Island to the public and used it for training flyers in the use of air-to-ground guided missiles.

"What do you say?" Spud asked impatiently.

Tommy hesitated, then took the plunge. "Sorry, Spud, but my mind is made up. I'm already com—"

"Listen to me, Tommy!" Spud was almost sobbing now. "I tell you, this is a *big deal.* A real ding-dong doozie-roo! In the first place—and this is top secret information, Tommy—my dad is behind this expedition. He wants to get a big scoop for the *News-Star,* and he's letting me be the reporter who handles the story. He says it's the biggest archaeological scoop since they uncovered King Tut back in 1922 in Egypt."

Tommy said, "I can't imagine your father sponsoring such a harebrained scheme. Hunting a pot of gold at the foot of the rainbow would make more sense, if you ask me."

Spud's sigh practically blew the receiver out of Tommy's hand.

"All right, all right—I had planned to tell you this in person when you got here, but if you're going to be stubborn, I'll have to play my aces, I guess.

"It's like this: The famous underwater movie photographer, Kurt Gerlock, was working on a big motion picture production over in the Mediterranean last winter, when he came across the logbook of a Spanish galleon, the *St. Regis.*

"Gerlock knew enough Spanish history to know that the king of Spain, back in 1580, had ordered the *St. Regis* to run up from Mexico and recover Cabrillo's bones from San Miguel Island and bring them back to Spain. According to the history books, the *St. Regis* was lost at sea and never seen again.

"That's where this logbook comes in. It proves that the *St. Regis* hit a rock and foundered in ten fathoms of water while attempting to enter the harbor on San Miguel. The ship sank so fast, all they saved was the logbook. The map showing where Cabrillo was buried went down with the galleon. That's why the grave has been lost for centuries.''

Tommy broke in skeptically, "Even if you found the wreck, wouldn't this map have disintegrated ages ago?''

"No,'' contradicted Spud. "The logbook says—and I've seen a photocopy of the page describing the wreck, Tommy, with my own two eyes— the map was carved on a sheet of lead and attached to the bulkhead of the captain's cabin. It's still there. It has to be. A diver can find it easily.''

Tommy was still unimpressed. "You've been looking at too many underwater TV thrillers, Spud. I'm surprised at you.''

"Oh yeah?'' Spud bridled. "Well, my father hates TV trash, and he thinks enough of Mr. Gerlock's logbook to risk one hundred thousand dollars to underwrite the deal!''

"Well, he can kiss that money good-by. The only one who'll profit is this Gerlock, selling his story for one hundred thousand dollars.''

Spud said stiffly, "Gerlock won't collect a penny until he has delivered the goods. In installments, at that. Dad pays him ten thousand dollars if the television camera positively locates the sunken hulk of the *St. Regis;* forty thousand dollars if the divers come up with the lead-plate map in good condition; and the remaining fifty thousand dollars if it leads them to Cabrillo's grave.''

Tommy was so intrigued by what Spud was saying that he forgot this call was costing him more money by the minute.

"This gets crazier by the minute, Spud,'' Tommy said jeeringly. "For the sake of argument, let's suppose your father invests one hundred thousand dollars and gets a human skeleton in return. How's he going to convince the Spanish government that it's the real McCoy? They won't pay off that half million dollar bounty without every scientific test in the world. You know that.''

Spud had a startling answer for that one.

"The Spanish government's leading archaeologist, Dr. Antonio Bonilla, who runs the big museum at Seville, is to act as judge. If he identifies the bones and armor as being authentic, Spain will pay off the five hundred thousand dollars. Dad would deduct his expenses and turn the rest over to the United Way and the Red Cross.''

"Dr. Antonio Bonilla?'' Tommy repeated. "Seems to me I've heard of him somewhere or other. Name sounds awfully familiar, anyway. Wonder if he's an exchange professor at Cal Tech or something?"

Spud replied, "I don't think so, but I can ask him. He's in the room next to mine, right this minute."

"Dr. Bonilla's in Santa Bonita?"

"Nowhere else, pal. Dad cabled him that we were going to make this expedition to San Miguel Island as soon as the Navy gave us a landing permit, so Dr. Bonilla flew over from Seville two weeks ago to be ready to go along. Dad picked him up at the Los Angeles International Airport and sneaked him up here under wraps. We can't let rival newspapers get wind of this, you know."

Taken somewhat aback, Tommy inquired, "Does Dr. Bonilla think Gerlock's logbook is genuine?"

"Not a doubt in the world, he says. You'll love him, Tommy. He lost an eye fighting with the British Army against Rommel's Afrika Korps in World War II. Speaks perfect English. I'm dying to have you two meet."

Spud's last remark snapped Tommy back to reality. The elapsed-time counter on his solar watch told him they had been yakking for nearly ten minutes. Money down the drain!

"Spud, let's QSY back to twenty meters now, huh? So you can phonepatch me through to my folks?"

"They've gone to Beverly Hills for the weekend and won't be back till Tuesday. When will you get here, Tommy? We don't leave Stearn's Wharf until about ten Monday night, so as to reach the island Tuesday daylight. The Navy's only giving us three days before the missiles start raining down again."

Tommy said, "During those three days I'll be climbing glaciers in the Cascade Mountains, pal. When I get back we can compare notes via ham radio. Good luck with your Cabrillo hunt, old man, and seventy-three for now."

He hung up without giving Spud a chance to argue any further with him. To be truthful about it, Tommy was so intrigued by the idea of diving for phantom galleons off San Miguel Island that he was afraid he might weaken and accept Spud's invitation.

Back at his packing, Tommy mumbled to himself, "Dr. Bonilla...Dr. Bonilla. Why does that name seem so familiar to me?"

Then it dawned on him. Night before last, at a friend's hamshack here in Ocean Park, Tommy had talked to a Spanish ham in Seville on fifteen meter phone. The Spaniard's name was Antonio—and he was an archaeologist in charge of a big museum in Seville!

Some vague sense of uneasiness sent Tommy to the next room to consult his Uncle JC's copy of *Amateur Wireless Biographical Directory,* a British publication that gave short sketches on European radio hams.

By international agreement, each country in the world was assigned identifying call letters for radio and TV stations. The letters W, K, N and A had been assigned to the United States of America. Continental Spain, Tommy knew, was EA. He couldn't remember what Antonio's call sign was, but he was sure he would find it in the British directory.

Looking under Spain, he found what he was looking for:

EA7WK—Antonio Bonilla, operator. QTH: Plaza Vieja 39, Sevilla. Museum curator. Europe's leading authority on arms and armour. Lost left eye fighting with British near Tobruk in World War II. Catholic. Unmarried. PhD., Univ. of Madrid. Active in Amateur Radio since 1937. Single sideband only since 1968.

The listing went on to give the many awards and honors that Dr. Bonilla had won in the field of Amateur Radio, including being the first Spaniard to bounce a VHF signal off the moon, and two winters at the South Pole as an IGY observer.

Since high-powered amplifiers and large beam antennas were out of reach of Tommy Rockford's wallet, he was not familiar with the big-name operators in the single-sideband DX realm of ham radio; but he remembered now that Lyle Stark, his host at station W7RDR here in town, had referred to "Tony" Bonilla as one of his regular on-the-air friends.

Tommy's sun-bronzed cheeks went pale as his thoughts probed deeper into this amazing coincidence of names. Could there be two Dr. Antonio Bonillas, both serving the same museum in Seville, and both of them minus a left eye as a result of desert fighting?

If not, then how could Dr. Bonilla have been talking to him from Seville two nights ago, when Spud Kleveland said he had been in California for the past two weeks?

One or the other had to be an impostor—and the quickest way

to solve the mystery would be for Tommy to get on the air with W7RDR's big station tonight and see if he could work EA7WK.

DX contacts were thrilling in themselves, but tonight Tommy Rockford had a strong premonition that DX would bring danger as well, if his talk with EA7WK proved that the Dr. Bonilla in Santa Bonita was a swindler after Mr. Kleveland's $100,000!

CHAPTER THREE

"CALLING CQ SPAIN!"

A rriving at W7RDR's home near Ocean Park's famous Sunset View arch overlooking the beach, Tommy was dismayed to find no one at home. Then he remembered that Lyle Stark was taking his family to a movie.

Such was the informality and close-knit friendship existing among radio hams everywhere that Stark, who had only met Tommy at a transmitter hunt picnic a month ago, had given the California teenager a standing invitation to use his station in his absence.

Etched against the stars some eighty feet above the roof of the Stark home was W7RDR's triband beam antenna, which could be rotated to direct a radio signal to any part of the world. That was a comforting thought to Tommy as he entered the unlocked house, switched on a light and made his way upstairs to W7RDR's deluxe hamshack.

Lyle Stark was too busy running his oyster cannery to build his own equipment, so he bought the best commercial gear available. The transceiver was an ICOM IC-751 driving a one and a half kilowatt amplifier—the most powerful signal squirter allowed by the law—which Tommy dreamed of owning someday.

High power, of itself, was not too important in the world of ham radio. Tommy had worked more than a hundred foreign stations to qualify for his DX Century Club and WAC, or Worked All Continents awards, with one-hundred watts of power. But tonight, wanting to work into Spain at a season of the year when radio conditions were not at their best, it was comforting to know that he had a "full gallon," as hams called operating with the maximum legal power, to punch a solid signal through the QRM. And because of the signal-focusing capabilities of the beam antenna, he had the equivalent of several kilowatts of power.

While the rig was warming up, Tommy set about the various steps necessary to prepare for an attempt at a long-distance radio contact with a precise spot on the surface of the globe. For a general call he would put out a "CQ" and answer anyone who came back to him. But working into a specific city six thousand miles away could not be done by slipshod methods or guesswork.

His first step was to establish the Great Circle bearing to determine the shortest possible air-line distance between Ocean Park, Washington, and Seville, Spain. On the wall above W7RDR's operating bench was a Great Circle World Map, with a thumbtack marking the location of Lyle Stark's station, just north of the mouth of the Columbia River between Oregon and Washington.

A string attached to this thumbtack enabled Tommy to line up the shortest signal path to Seville, Spain.

His findings would have puzzled any student who was used to the flat Mercator Projection map of the world as shown in a geography book. On a flat map, a string stretched between Washington State and Spain would run easterly across the United States, touching such cities as Butte, Montana; Milwaukee, Wisconsin; and Boston, Massachusetts.

But Tommy's Great Circle string indicated that the actual shortest distance between Ocean Park and Seville was at an angle of 44°, or almost exactly northeast, forming a line that crossed Hudson's Bay and Labrador as it curved across the Atlantic.

All Tommy had to do to beam his radio signal into Spain tonight was to set the compass dial pointer of the antenna rotor to 44° and press a control button. A selsyn motor at the top of the antenna tower, synchronized with a matching selsyn in the rotator control box on Stark's desk, automatically swung the beam around to bear exactly on Seville, six thousand miles away.

That done, Tommy carefully checked the ALC and collector current readings on the ICOM, gently tapped on the mike to check modulation, and found everything ready to go.

One thing disturbed him tonight—the time difference between

his station and Dr. Bonilla's EA7WK. It was 9 PM Pacific Time in Ocean Park, which meant it was five o'clock tomorrow morning in Seville. Even though radio hams—especially DX men like Dr. Bonilla—were notorious night owls, there was very little chance that he would find EA7WK scanning the band at this hour of the day.

Tommy put on the "cans," or headphones, and had a quick listen over the single-sideband portion of the fifteen-meter band, which he recalled Lyle Stark's telling him was Dr. Bonilla's favorite spot on the radio spectrum.

The first signal he heard was a GM3 in Edinburgh, Scotland, in a friendly roundtable with a CN8 in French Morocco and a ZB2 in Gibraltar.

"At least the path is open to the part of the world I want to get into," Tommy muttered with relief. He tuned across the band again until he picked up a single-sideband station in Portugal signing CT1VJ. The Portuguese was in QSO with a ham in Cadiz, a Spanish city not too far from Seville. Conditions, then, were excellent for a try into Dr. Bonilla's home QTH.

Tuning the frequency synthesizer of the transceiver a few kilohertz away from CT1VJ's frequency, so as not to cause QRM, Tommy tuned his antenna to the same slot and settled back to begin his fishing.

It was not necessary to manually switch from send to receive, or vice versa, with W7RDR's fancy equipment; the vibrations of Tommy's voice activated relays to put the transmitter on the air, and when he paused between words, the voice break-in equipment automatically switched back to the receiver.

In a clear, distinct voice, Tommy began chanting the familiar "DX mating call" so dear to radio hams the world over: "CQ Spain, CQ Spain, CQ Spain...this is W7RDR in Ocean Park, Washington, USA, with K6ATX at the mike, calling CQ Spain and standing by for a call..."

It was Tommy's practice to call CQ for one minute and listen for an answer for the next minute or so. Tonight, he got plenty of responses, but from operators in Egypt, Denmark and Turkey. Since he had specified Spain in his call, he ignored these "eager beaver DX hounds" whose only desire was a DX contact.

Shifting frequency to another nearby open spot on the band, Tommy now changed his call to pinpoint his desired location: "CQ Seville, Spain—CQ Seville, Spain... this is W7RDR, calling any amateur station in Seville, Spain..."

He hardly hoped for an answer, but luck was with him. He had just begun scanning the band for a reply when EA7JQ came back with the good word that he was Isidoro Navaro Moreno of Sevilla, reading Tommy five by five—a fairly good signal report. EA7JQ, by contrast, was a weak three by two, although a slight swing of the beam antenna built Isidoro's signal up to three by five, a faint but readable signal.

"Many thanks, Isidoro," Tommy said after exchanging the usual signal data. "It is most urgent, *amigo,* that I get in touch with a Dr. Antonio Bonilla of 39 Plaza Viejo in your city. His call is EA7WK, repeat EA7WK. Could you telephone him and ask him to get on this frequency, please?"

Isidoro came back instantly, "*Si, si*—I know Dr. Bonilla very well, Tomás. He was on the air earlier tonight, working Thule in northern Greenland. But it is just getting daylight here in Sevilla, Tomas. Are you sure you wish me to disturb him at this hour?"

Tommy's heart was slamming his ribs. He knew that at any moment the signal might fade completely out. Conditions were best when signals traveled a path in darkness.

"I know it's a terrible hour to disturb him, Isidoro, but this is very urgent. Please help me!"

There was such a long pause that Tommy was afraid the band had gone out. Then EA7JQ came back, obviously reluctant to make a telephone call at this hour of the morning, his time:

"*Esta bueno,* I will telephone him. QRX."

QRX meant "standby, please," in any language.

The sweep-second hand on the big twenty-four hour clock on W7RDR's hamshack wall made five complete circuits of the dial before EA7JQ's pleasant Latin accents again sounded in Tommy's headphones.

"I have Dr. Antonio Bonilla tuning up on this frequency, Tomás," Isidoro said. "I hope it is really important, this QSO. His landlord was very angry at me for rousing him so early to go wake up EA7WK. What he said about Amateur Radio was most—how you say it in English?—uncomplimentary."

Tommy was blushing furiously as he said, "I can't thank you enough, Isidoro." Then, realizing that Dr. Bonilla was probably listening to their conversation while he tuned up his own transmitter, Tommy went on, "If you copy me, Dr. Bonilla, this is K6ATX calling from

Washington State, USA. You may remember our QSO earlier in the week, via W7RDR.''

Tommy could hear the hum and crackle of static blending with the characteristic flutter of short wave radio. Then the well-remembered voice of Tony Bonilla came loud and clear, indicating that he was running twice the power of Isidoro:

"*Buenas dias,* friend Tom. Do not apologize for awakening me—I was planning to attend six o'clock Mass anyway. How are you this fine morning?''

Tommy wasn't sure if there was any sarcasm implied in his emphasis of the word "morning" or if he imagined it.

"Doctor—Tony—I have reason to believe that an impostor using your name is down in California on a scientific expedition, claiming to represent your Museum of the Indies in Seville. It involves the five hundred thousand dollar bounty your government is offering for the discovery of Juan Rodriguez Cabrillo's remains—''

When Tommy paused for breath he distinctly heard Dr. Bonilla's startled gasp.

"*Caramba!* This is most disturbing news to me, Don Tomas!'' EA7WK exclaimed. "It sounds as if Lou Weber is working again!''

"Lou Weber?'' Tommy echoed. "Who's he?''

"Lou Weber,'' said EA7WK, "is the real name of an international confidence man and jewel thief, Tomas. He specializes in swindling the wealthy by selling them counterfeit *objets d'art,* spurious Old Masters, and the like.''

"What makes you think Lou Weber may be the man who seems to be impersonating you down in California?''

"Because on a previous occasion Weber used a forged passport bearing my name, taking advantage of my position in the field of early Spanish history,'' Dr. Bonilla said. His excited voice was barely getting through the atmospherics now, as sunrise in Spain began to close the band. Tommy had to strain his ears and adjust the fine-tuning controls of the ICOM's receiver to maximum efficiency to get Dr. Bonilla's fading voice:

"...wanted by the law on both sides...Atlantic. Tomás, amigo—if I should arrange...take a jet flight to the States...investigate this matter...since you are not in Santa Bonita...whom do I contact in California?''

Tommy said, "Your signal's way down in the mud now, Doctor.

Get in touch with my friend Sheriff Ross Jackson at the courthouse in Santa Bonita. Did you get that, Doctor?"

Whisper-faint came EA7WK's fading signal: *"Si*—I QSL as follows: Sheriff Ross Jackson...Santa Bonita courthouse...Do not let Lou Weber get away this time..."

At that moment Dr. Bonilla's voice was completely blanked out by a powerful signal from Japan, off the back of Stark's beam, and exactly on their frequency. Tommy knew he would be unable to resume his QSO with Spain now, even to thank Isidoro for his role in establishing the contact.

Tommy was drenched with perspiration as he pulled the big switch to put W7RDR off the air. He opened Lyle Stark's logbook to enter the transmission.

Another thought came to Tommy. Whenever radio hams worked DX they exchanged "QSL cards" in confirmation. W7RDR kept his QSL cards in files arranged alphabetically by world radio zones, in contrast with the practice of many hams—K6ATX among them—of papering the hamshack walls with QSLs.

It took only a moment for Tommy to locate W7RDR's file for the EA7 call zone. It contained a dozen or so QSL cards from Spanish stations Lyle had worked in the past. One, bearing a date three months old, was marked EA7WK in large red letters. In addition to a description of Dr. Bonilla's radio equipment, it carried a photographed portrait of the operator he had just been talking to.

Tommy found himself studying Dr. Bonilla's picture with keenest interest. EA7WK was bald as an egg. He wore a plastic patch over his left eyesocket. His spiked mustache and pointed goatee made him resemble a Spanish conquistador of old.

On impulse, Tommy put the QSL card into his pocket for further use. Finding a scratch pad, he jotted a note to W7RDR:

DEAR OM,
    Had an emergency come up, had to borrow UR rig, many TNX. Am borrowing EA7WK's QSL card but will return safely.
    Am leaving for Portland tonight to catch plane for California to handle an emergency situation. Will give you a shout from home station later in week.
VY 73, K6ATX

Ten minutes later Tommy was toting his mountain-climbing gear back into his uncle's beach cottage. His Mt. Rainier expedition with the Sierra Club gang was now crowded completely out of his thoughts.

Still later, driving down the North Shore Highway of the Columbia River toward Portland, Oregon, and the nearest airport, Tommy wondered if he shouldn't have handled this thing with a telephone call to his friend, Sheriff Ross Jackson.

But if Spud's father was being victimized by an international crook, the high adventure of exposing the conspiracy might prove to be even more exciting than climbing a mountain peak—and perhaps even more dangerous.

At three o'clock the following afternoon, the limousine from the Santa Bonita municipal airport dropped Tommy Rockford off in front of his parents' Channel Cities Travel Agency office on State Street. Since it was Sunday, the office was closed; but Tommy's telephone call from the airport had brought Spud Kleveland to meet him here. Too young to drive a car, Spud got around on a foreign-made moped.

Spud's eyes were shining with excitement behind his horn-rimmed glasses as he rushed over to pump Tommy's hand.

"You sure play mean practical jokes, Tommy," Spud jabbered. "Making me think over the telephone you weren't interested in our galleon hunt. I almost cried, I was so disappointed."

Tommy said, "Let's go into Dad's office a minute, Spud. I want to show you something."

"Sure thing, Tommy. We're expecting you over at our place for lunch, and to meet Mr. Gerlock and Dr. Bonilla. I'm glad you flew down instead of drove. You'd have arrived bushed."

Tommy unlocked his father's office with the key he always carried, and a moment later was shutting the door against the noise of traffic and the possibility of being overheard.

Spud was jabbering excitedly; "We're going over to the islands on a crane barge Dad leased from an oil company. By leaving after dark nobody will notice. You'd think Cabrillo's bones were more valuable than atom bomb secrets, all the security measures Dad's taking to make sure no rival newspapers get wind of what's going on. . . What have you got to show me, Tommy?"

From an inside pocket of his Patagonia jacket Tommy produced the QSL card he had borrowed the night before from W7RDR's files. He handed it to Spud with the comment, "Ever see this guy before?"

Spud took one look and said, "Why, sure—that's Dr. Bonilla! I never knew he was a radio ham, too!"

CHAPTER FOUR

FRIENDS OR CRIMINALS?

Confusion showed on Tommy's face. Spud's answer was not what he had expected it to be. His impulsive flight back to California—squandering a goodly portion of his precious summer vacation allowance—had been based on the assumption that the Dr. Bonilla he would find here in Santa Bonita would bear no physical resemblance to the one on the QSL card from Spain.

Now he was faced with the disquieting possibility that the voice he had assumed was that of the real Dr. Bonilla belonged to some imposter bootlegging EA7WK's ham call!

He said to Spud, "He didn't tell you he is one of the most active DX operators in Europe?"

"No, he didn't let on he knew a thing about hamming when I showed him my gear at WA6IBR the day he got here!"

Tommy tugged thoughtfully at an ear lobe. Then he said, "What kind of a guy is Kurt Gerlock? Friendly, I mean?"

"Oh, sure. Most interesting man I ever met, in fact. He has an irritating habit of tacking 'see?' onto the end of every other sentence, but that doesn't mean anything."

Tommy took the QSL card back from Spud. "My friend," he said, "brace yourself for a shock. I had a QSO with Dr. Bonilla in Seville, Spain, at nine-fifteen last night up in Ocean Park."

It took a moment for Spud to digest the significance of Tommy's statement.

"But you couldn't have!" the boy exclaimed. "We took Dr. Bonilla to his first drive-in movie theater last night!"

Tommy grinned bleakly. "Now you know why I dropped everything to fly home. I wanted to find out how Dr. Antonio Bonilla could be talking to me via ham radio from Spain and be your house guest in California at the same time. One of the two has to be an impostor...and I'm inclined to think the phoney is the one who's your house guest."

Spud's cheeks slowly drained of color as Tommy told him about Lou Weber, the swindler who was wanted by the police of two continents—a confidence man who had previously impersonated Dr. Antonio Bonilla, the scientist.

When Tommy had finished, Spud said in a scared voice, "I remember now how strangely he acted when I asked him to talk to somebody over my station. He said it would be too dangerous to let anyone know he was even in America—that Mr. Gerlock and my father had sworn him to secrecy."

Tommy replaced the QSL card in his jacket pocket. "Before you drive me out to your place," he said, "I'd like to drop in at the Western Union office and find out for sure whether anyone sent a cable to Spain asking Dr. Bonilla to visit California and identify Cabrillo's bones, if and when they were found. Maybe Gerlock just pretended to send a cable."

Spud shook his head. "Mr. Gerlock didn't send the cable. My father did. I was there when he telephoned it to the operator, with Mr. Gerlock listening also. And I read the cable Dr. Bonilla sent back from Spain, telling what jet flight he would be on when we met him at the airport in LA."

This mysterious business was getting more complicated by the minute.

"Well," Tommy said, "if your father actually sent a cable to Spain, and it was answered from Spain, then it leaves us with two riddles. First, who was I talking to in Seville last night? And second, why did your Dr. Bonilla pretend he knew nothing about ham radio, when he's one of Europe's foremost operators? Unless he's Lou Weber, made up to look like Dr. Bonilla in a physical sense, but knew he couldn't possibly impersonate a radio ham well enough to convince another radio ham?"

Spud was trembling as they locked up the office and went back to where the moped waited at the curb. He said, "I-I feel all sick at the stomach like I did the time Jigger O'Dell pointed his gun at us and stuffed us into the trunk of his car."

Tommy stood by while Spud lashed his canvas traveling bag to the luggage rack of the scooter. "Let's analyze this thing," he said. "The key to the final payoff in this whole business is whether an official representative of Spain—Dr. Antonio Bonilla—will certify that a certain human skeleton buried on San Miguel Island is actually Cabrillo's. Right?"

"Right."

"Okay. What is to prevent Lou Weber from going into partnership with a deep-sea diving expert named Gerlock and planting a confederate in Seville to intercept any mail or cables addressed to Dr. Bonilla?"

Spud took off his glasses and polished them. "That sounds like something out of a corny cloak-and-dagger TV plot, Tommy."

"But remember," Tommy pointed out, "that Gerlock and Bonilla are playing for high stakes—one hundred thousand dollars. Their success depends on the cooperation of a scientist who will arrive in the States by jet from Spain and identify a human skeleton that Gerlock could conceivably have planted ahead of time on San Miguel Island."

Spud's lower lip started to quiver. "B-But Gerlock won't get paid off unless he discovers a sunken Manila galleon, and locates the chart that's supposed to be in the captain's cabin. You don't think they could dream up a sunken Spanish galleon, do you?"

No, Tommy was forced to confess, he didn't. If the underwater television camera located a phantom galleon off the shores of San Miguel Island, the mystery would really begin to thicken.

"If this thing turned out to be a hoax," Spud quavered, "it would make Dad the laughingstock of the newspaper world, wouldn't it? Even if he didn't lose any money...Tommy, we've got to figure this thing out. Don't you think we ought to ask Ross Jackson what to do?"

Tommy said, "That's exactly what I was about to suggest—and there's no time like the present. Sunday afternoon is when the sheriff tries to catch up on his private correspondence and we might find him in."

A two-minute ride brought them to Santa Bonita's unique courthouse—famed the world over as a replica of a Moorish castle in Spain. When they presented themselves at Sheriff Ross Jackson's office in the jail building, they found him working on his private correspondence, exactly as Tommy had hoped.

"Tommy!" exclaimed the sheriff, rising from his desk. "I thought you were up in Washington this summer!"

"I was," Tommy said, "but an emergency has come up that brought me home, Ross. Spud and I need your help."

"Then have a chair, help yourselves to a Coke from the machine there, and tell Uncle Ross your troubles."

Ross Jackson had been a bomber pilot in Vietnam. Long active in Boy Scouting and Little League Baseball in Santa Bonita, he had been Tommy's pal and confidant since grade-school days.

Without further ado, Tommy plunged directly into his story, Sheriff Jackson jotting down notes at frequent intervals. When Tommy had finished, Jackson was silent for a considerable period, pondering the various baffling angles of the case.

"I've heard of Lou Weber, the society swindler, of course," Jackson mused, "although to my knowledge he has never worked the West Coast. I'll have the FBI send me their dossier on him...Spud, stop blubbering. Your father isn't a sucker for falling for Weber's line—assuming, of course, that your Dr. Bonilla is actually Lou Weber. Confidence men always swear their victims to secrecy—and in your father's case, secrecy was the essence of the whole thing, if his newspaper was to get a scoop."

Jackson lit up a pipe and took a turn or two around the room. Then he wheeled on Tommy and said, "Dr. Bonilla is flying out from Spain to investigate this impostor, did you say?"

"He didn't make it definite," Tommy answered, "and the band was beginning to fade out, but he did QSL what I told him about contacting you when he got to Santa Bonita. Of course, I can't be positive I was talking to the real Dr. Bonilla in Seville, since Spud has identified the photo on the QSL card as his guest."

After another long interval of study, Sheriff Jackson said, "Tell you what, fellows. We don't have enough positive evidence yet for me to make an arrest for conspiracy to defraud. Suppose we play this by ear. Go ahead and pay your visit to San Miguel. You won't turn up a sunken galleon, of course, but Gerlock may try to wheedle Mr. Kleveland into paying off on the pretext that some rock or other sunken wreckage is the *St. Regis.*"

Tommy said, "I can take my two-meter gear along and report to you by ham radio. The Navy's only allowing us three days on the missile range anyway."

The sheriff shook his head to that suggestion. "Let's leave ham radio out of this. Your barge will be equipped with a radio-telephone. If you need to contact me, do it via ship-to-shore. Meanwhile, I'll have the FBI see what we can find on both Gerlock and Lou Weber."

Feeling better for having taken Ross Jackson into their confidence, the two boys left the courthouse by a freight elevator—to avoid having to explain Tommy's return from the north to every deputy they met—and a few minutes later they were speeding along the palm-lined ocean boulevard toward suburban Montecito, where the Kleveland estate was located.

Spud's father, as the millionaire publisher of the only daily newspaper in the county seat, was a man of tremendous influence in community affairs. His vast wealth also made him a logical target for swindlers and con men.

Spud turned the moped into the long, curving driveway that looped up the slope toward the stately Mediterranean villa that was his home. The boys dismounted behind a large, marble fountain in front of the mansion.

Out on a sun terrace Tommy saw Chester Kleveland, Spud's father, engaged in conversation with two guests. Tommy recognized Dr. Bonilla instantly, from his picture on EA7WK's QSL card. Kurt Gerlock was wearing a yachting cap and brass-buttoned coat, a garb common to Santa Bonita's boating set.

"Listen, Spud," Tommy said under his breath, "whatever you do, don't bring up ham radio in front of Dr. Bonilla. If he's really Lou Weber, that would scare him out of our trap."

"I won't," Spud promised. "I—I'm scared of him."

A moment later Mr. Kleveland was hailing them as the two boys headed up the marble steps of the terrace.

Tommy's first impression of Kurt Gerlock was neither favorable nor unfavorable. The man had a broad, jack-o'-lantern smile that exposed every tooth in his head—a smile Tommy was to learn that had nothing to do with amusement or good humor, but was in the nature of a permanent grimace.

Gerlock stood a head shorter than Tommy. His hair was gray and curly as fleece, and he had the thick-corded neck and blocky shoulders of a TV wrestler. Underwater motion picture photography was his profession, and the work had burned his skin to an oiled bronze tone.

Dr. Bonilla, upon closer view, bore a striking resemblance to the picture on the QSL card, Tommy observed as they headed up the stairway toward the men on the terrace, but he was not the same man. This Dr. Bonilla had too much hair, although he was partially bald, and his cheeks were fleshier, giving him the look of a Falstaff rather than a Spanish cavalier.

"Well, if it isn't Tommy, back from the frozen north!" boomed Chester Kleveland, greeting Tommy with a handshake. "I'm sorry you had to miss your Sierra Club adventure, Tommy, but I promise you our little junket to San Miguel Island will be equally exciting, and Mt. Rainier will always be there. Now I want to present my house guests and our partners in adventure—Dr. Antonio Bonilla of Seville, the distinguished archaeologist, and Kurt Gerlock, the famous underwater cameraman whose movies have thrilled us for years."

Everyone mumbled polite responses. Dr. Bonilla's handclasp was so soft and moist it reminded Tommy of wet bologna. His greeting was so effusive and so charged with continental charm that Tommy found himself forgetting the sinister question mark that shadowed the situation.

"So this is Tommy Rockford!" beamed Kurt Gerlock over a vigorous handshake. "Young man, you're more famous than you know. Last winter I was working on a picture over in London. I tuned in a BBC newscast and heard about your exploit with the gangsters who kidnapped you and Spud here, and how you sent out an SOS at midnight with some kind of a radio gadget and saved both of your lives."

"That's right, sir!" chimed in Spud. "Tommy is the bravest, smartest guy who ever lived."

Tommy squirmed with embarrassment. His "SOS at midnight" adventure of last winter was one he would never live down, and Spud was his most loyal press agent.*

"Anyway," Kurt Gerlock said, "we're mighty glad you got back to California in time to join the expedition, Tommy. Welcome aboard."

At that moment a white-jacketed Filipino servant appeared to an-

---

*See *SOS At Midnight*, ARRL, 1985

nounce that luncheon was being served on the South Terrace.

"Shall we go hang on the nose bag?" asked Mr. Kleveland, who despite the elegance of his home surroundings, was never a man to put on airs. "While we're eating, Tommy, Mr. Gerlock can explain how he first got on the track of the phantom galleon of San Miguel Island."

CHAPTER FIVE

LEAF FROM A LOGBOOK

K urt Gerlock was talking about his life as a movie cameraman almost before the five of them had been ushered to their seats on the terrace overlooking Santa Barbara Channel, with the islands—San Miguel among them—lying on the horizon.

During the course of a long career—Gerlock was past sixty now—he had shot motion pictures all over the world, high in the clouds and under the sea, including below the Polar ice cap. In the second World War he had been a member of a US Navy UDT, or Underwater Demolition Team, and had received several decorations for his exploits as a frogman, blowing up enemy ships in Toulon and Cherbourg harbors.

Mention of the war caused Gerlock to nod his head in the direction of Dr. Bonilla, who had not uttered a word to anyone since his introduction to Tommy.

"Doc here knows what war is like, too," Gerlock said. "Tony lost that eye durin' the seige of Tobruk in 'forty-one, see? Tell Tommy about it Doc. You got a hero's medal out of it."

Dr. Bonilla smiled modestly. "A medal, she is pretty to look at, but the left eye, I prefer to keep, no? Let us say I do not wish to talk about the war, Señores."

Tommy made no comment, hoping the conversation would veer away from Gerlock's bragging and center on their forthcoming hunt for the sunken hulk of the galleon *St. Regis*. But the movie photographer got sidetracked on a long discourse about a pearling expedition to the South Seas, and it finally took Mr. Kleveland to get him onto the subject of Cabrillo's lost grave.

"Tommy didn't know about our Spanish galleon project until I gave Spud permission to telephone him the news this week." The publisher took advantage of a pause when Gerlock was washing down some fried chicken with iced coffee. "I think we would all enjoy hearing again how you first got a clue to the galleon off San Miguel, and how you met Dr. Bonilla here."

"That would be most interesting indeed," Tommy said dryly, with a hidden meaning that was understood only by Spud.

Gerlock wiped his greasy mouth with the back of his hand, helped himself to a succulent breast of chicken, which he began shredding with his stubby fingers, and launched into his new topic with gusto, tucking morsels of food into his cheeks each time he paused for breath.

"It was this way, Tommy," Gerlock said. "Last year I was workin' as first assistant cameraman for Majestic Pictures Corporation, see? We were shootin' underwater stuff off the Mediterranean coast of Spain, with Sammy Vozarski directin'.

"Durin' my off time, no matter where I find myself in the world, I make a habit of hangin' around waterfronts, swappin' lies with old salts, especially divers like I used to be. So in this saloon in Barcelona, I make friends with an old barnacle named Primo Ruiz, see? He was a Minorcan, and had learned how to play poker from the GIs durin' the war.

"Well," Gerlock continued, "I know a few tricks with a poker deck myself, so first thing you know, Ruiz was up to the Gypsy rings in his ears with IOUs to me, see? That was when he told me he had an old ship's logbook in his sea chest, a logbook that belonged to one of the old Manila treasure galleons in the fifteen hundreds, and that this one had a clue to buried treasure on the last page.

"Heck, every codger you run into, every beachcomber you meet, can show you a genu-wine pirate treasure map at the drop of a hat. Usually they'll swap it for the price of a drink, see? But I knew we had our picture in the can and would be shovin' off for Hollywood to shoot the interiors before Ruiz ever paid off his gamblin' debts, so to humor the old buzzard, I told him to show me this logbook he wanted to swap for my IOUs."

Spud Kleveland whispered to Tommy, "Doesn't he remind you of the old sea captain in *Treasure Island,* Tommy?"

"Anyhow," Gerlock went on, chewing chicken all the while, "the minute I laid eyes on this logbook I got the feeling maybe the old gaffer had somethin'. Ruiz said his grandfather a couple of dozen generations back had been skipper of a Manila galleon, the *St. Regis,* see?

"So I wound up swappin' my IOU collection for his logbook, and a week or so later when we were filming stock shots in Seville, I took the logbook over to the government museum to get it appraised. You'd of thought I had brought in the Holy Grail, they got so excited. They sent for their boss to come and have a look, and that, Tommy, is how I first met Doc Bonilla, see? And a lucky day it was for all of us, too."

The gentle-mannered Dr. Bonilla smiled sadly.

"Just think of it, Señores," he said ruefully. "For hundreds of years my museum had been searching for the missing logbook of the *St. Regis* galleon to add to its collection. And here it turned up in the sea chest of a drunkard from the Island of Minorca, for an Americano to win at a poker table. The irony of it!"

Spud, who had an irritating habit of wanting to show off his superior knowledge from time to time, butted in now to tell Tommy about the Manila galleons of the Sixteenth Century—how Spain permitted but one galleon per year to visit China and Manila to pick up priceless cargoes of silks, spices, gold, ivory and jewels. Finally, after about two centuries, pirates made the Pacific sea lanes too perilous for Spanish treasure shipments, and the Manila galleon era was ended.

"I know all that, Spud," Tommy said impatiently. "I got a B plus in European history, remember. Go on, Mr. Gerlock..."

"Well, the museum folks translated this logbook for me, see?" Gerlock resumed. "It was written in faded ink on parchment, in what they called archaic Spanish, so I couldn't decipher heads nor tails out of it.

"Anyway, it seems that in the year 1581, the King of Spain ordered the *St. Regis* to cruise up the coast from Mexico to the Isle of Possession off the coast of California—what we call San Miguel Island today—and pick up the mortal remains of Cabrillo, who had died there in 1543, see? Seems the king wanted Cabrillo brought back and entombed in a big cathedral, as befitted the discoverer of California, see?

"The men who buried Cabrillo had drawn a map of San Miguel Island—or rather, carved it with a knife on a sheet of soft lead—to show exactly where the grave was. The king turned this map over to the skipper of the *St. Regis,* and accordin' to the logbook, he had mounted it with screws or pegs to the bulkhead of his cabin in the poop of the ship, see?''

At this point Gerlock reached under his coat lapel for a bulging wallet, his thick fingers searching through a sheaf of cards for something to show Tommy.

"Anyway, the logbook said that when the galleon was tryin' to get into the harbor at San Miguel Island, a storm blew up and she drug her anchors and hit a big rock outside the bar, and sank with all hands. The skipper managed to save his logbook, but it was several years before he made it back home to the Island of Minorca in the Mediterranean Sea. The logbook stayed in the possession of his descendants and was forgotten until I come along and played poker with Primo Ruiz.''

Gerlock found what he had been searching for in his wallet, and handed it over for Tommy's inspection. It proved to be a photocopy of the last page of the *St. Regis'* logbook, bearing a date in 1581, thirty-eight years after the death of Cabrillo.

The only things Tommy could translate with the help of his high school Spanish were some latitude and longitude readings—120° 20' West, 34° 3' North. These bearings intersected on the precise location of San Miguel Island, which Tommy had only to lift his gaze to see on the hazy horizon to the southwest, some fifty miles distant from Santa Bonita.

"Doc Bonilla translated the words on that last page of the logbook in return for me selling the book to their museum,'' Gerlock went on. "It tells how the galleon sunk in ten fathom of water, at the foot of a rock shaped like a sugar-loaf, just outside the harbor bar, see?''

Tommy Rockford, who had done some exploring of desolate San Miguel Island himself, glanced up in excitement.

"The sugarloaf rock would be Sombrero Rock at the mouth of the Devil's Jaw inlet into Cuyler Harbor, wouldn't it? Because it looks like a Mexican's hat. I skin-dived for abalone there one summer before the Navy took the Island over for a bombing range.''

After Gerlock had stowed the photocopy back into his wallet as carefully as if it had been a thousand-dollar bill, he resumed. "Anyway, the logbook said they didn't salvage anything off the *St. Regis,* and it specifically mentioned having to report to the King of Spain the loss of the Cabrillo map, which had been left bolted to the bulkhead of the captain's cabin. I figger it's still there—the galleon, as well as the lead chart—and worth goin' after. So did Dr. Bonilla here, or he wouldn't have agreed to come all the way from Spain to pass judgment on Cabrillo's bones—if we found some."

After Gerlock had returned to California, he had paid a visit to Chester Kleveland, the newspaper publisher he figured would be most interested in the Cabrillo project on nearby San Miguel, in hopes that Kleveland could recommend some wealthy individual to underwrite the necessary expedition.

"I took one look at the photocopy of that galleon's logbook," Mr. Kleveland told Tommy, "and realized I had the most sensational archaeological story of the century in my very hands. So I agreed to subsidize Mr. Gerlock to the tune of one hundred thousand dollars, providing Dr. Bonilla would come over from Spain to confirm the authenticity of whatever bones we found."

A long silence followed, broken only by Kurt Gerlock's noisy slurping of his coffee. Finally Tommy said, "But why hasn't some diver stumbled onto that wrecked galleon in all these years? Sombrero Rock is only about a hundred yards offshore."

Mr. Kleveland said, "I wondered the same thing, but I'm told by the Navy that the kelp beds and the rip currents have kept skin divers away, and the Geodetic Survey doesn't make soundings that close to a visible shoal. And the fate of the *St. Regis* was lost to history until the Ruiz logbook turned up in Barcelona last year, remember."

Tommy had another point to raise: "Why do we have to be so hush-hush about this expedition if the Spanish government knows about the logbook? I'm surprised Spain didn't send an expedition over to San Miguel to hunt for the galleon."

The taciturn Dr. Bonilla answered that one.

"Mr. Gerlock would not sell the logbook to the Museum of the Indies unless the government gave him the exclusive—how you say— franchise to salvage the Cabrillo chart."

Everything seemed logical and plausible to Tommy now—Mr. Kleveland's willingness to finance the expedition, and his willingness to pay heavily for exclusive news coverage in the event the sensational discovery was actually made.

"You look skeptical, Tommy," chuckled Mr. Kleveland. "I admit it all sounds like a fairy tale. But Dr. Bonilla was willing to fly out from Spain at his own expense to join us, he's so convinced we have something."

"I'm not skeptical," Tommy said. "It's just that after more than four hundred years, I doubt if anything is left of the *St. Regis,* that's all. And it will be risking a diver's life in those dangerous waters to find out."

"We'll let underwater television do the exploring," Mr. Kleveland pointed out. "Once the galleon is located—"

At that moment Mr. Kleveland was interrupted by the approach of a servant, before whom their project could not be discussed.

Tommy had hung his jacket over the back of his chair at the outset of the luncheon, and as the servant leaned forward to clear away the dishes he accidentally brushed the jacket onto the tile floor.

When he stooped to retrieve the garment, something white fell out of an inside pocket and landed near Mr. Kleveland. Tommy saw with horror that what their host was leaning down to recover was EA7WK's ham radio QSL card bearing Dr. Bonilla's picture.

CHAPTER SIX

K6ATX PLANS STRATEGY

In the act of handing the telltale QSL card back to Tommy, Chester Kleveland recognized what it was and commented, "I see you've been working some nice DX again, eh? I wish I had time to take up the hobby my—Great Scott—what's this? What's Dr. Bonilla's picture doing on this card? He isn't a ham!"

Tommy and Spud exchanged sick glances as they saw Mr. Kleveland hand the card across the table to his Spanish guest. Dr. Bonilla, staring at his own likeness on the postcard with the Sevilla postmark, seemed for a moment to turn to stone.

"I had no idea you were a radio ham, Doctor," Mr. Kleveland said in astonishment. "Did you know it, Spud?"

Spud, white as a sheet, shook his head, mumbled something and pretended to drop his napkin under the table, so as to keep his frightened face out of sight.

For the barest fraction of a second Tommy saw—or imagined he saw—the raw shine of fear in Dr. Bonilla's one brown eye. Then, with melodious accents of pure Andalusian Spanish, he said, "This coincidence is easily explained, amigos. You confuse me with my, uh, young nephew, Tony. He is an Amateur Radio enthusiast."

Tommy's pulses were pounding. "He has the same name as yours?"

"*Si*—it is a common name in Spain. He lives at the Old Plaza in Seville. By a curious coincidence he, too, lost an eye—but in a fishing accident, not a war injury like mine."

Mr. Kleveland, unaware of the crosscurrents of drama all about him, said "You look enough alike to be twins."

Dr. Bonilla's fingers were drumming the glass table top, but otherwise he gave no outward signs of tension.

"The eye patch and the beard give that illusion, perhaps, but we are actually quite dissimilar."

"Is he an archaeologist?" Tommy inquired, remembering what the British directory had to say about EA7WK being a museum curator and Europe's outstanding authority on Spanish arms and armor.

Dr. Bonilla said easily, "Tony works as a taxidermist in my museum, but that is as far as it goes. Amateur Radio is his main interest."

Tommy flashed a cryptic glance at Spud. If Gerlock's companion was an impostor, there was one facet of the real Dr. Bonilla's character he could not fake—the hobby of ham radio. Hams talked a jargon both unique and technical. No one could pretend to be a radio ham unless he was one, except possibly a veteran shortwave listener.

The servant was bringing the dessert tray when Mr. Kleveland signaled for silence. After the servant had left, Spud's father said, "You understand, Tommy, that either we are on the verge of a very important discovery or else we face a total flop. In either event it would be catastrophic for the *News-Star* if word of this expedition leaked out prematurely. So I must swear you to absolute secrecy, Tommy, until this is all behind us, one way or the other."

Tommy grinned and crossed his heart with a fingertip.

"I swear not to breathe a word," he said. "As a matter of fact, I'm going to be one of those eat-and-run guests, Mr. Kleveland. I didn't get much sleep on the plane last night, so I'm going home and hit the sack."

Kleveland nodded somberly. "I'm glad you'll be incommunicado while you're in town, Tommy, because the paper carried a story about the Sierra Club mountaineering expedition this week and mentioned that you were joining the group at Mt. Rainier."

As soon as they had finished eating, Gerlock and Dr. Bonilla asked to be excused and retired to their rooms. "That QSL card must have been a bombshell for both of them," Tommy thought, "but Dr. Bonilla parried it very well. He almost convinced me I had been talking with a nephew by the same name."

Spud broke into his thoughts by asking him if he was acquainted with Ed Morin, W6SNI, who ran the Moright Marine Electronics firm on lower Delavina Street.

"Do I know him?" chuckled Tommy. "He's the guy who taught me how to skin dive and later graduated me to scuba. Why?"

"Because Ed's going to be operating the remote-controlled submarine tractor with the TV camera on it," Spud explained. "Ed uses it to help oil companies locate lost equipment when they're drilling for offshore oil, so Dad figured it would come in handy for locating the *St. Regis* at the foot of Sombrero Rock."

Tommy said, "You were lucky to get such a trustworthy man as Ed, Mr. Kleveland. I understand he's one of the best underwater television experts this side of Seattle."

Mr. Kleveland said, "I swore him to secrecy, just as I did you...I'll send a car to pick you up around dusk tomorrow, Tommy. The crane barge that's going to take us to San Miguel will be leaving Stearn's Wharf as soon as it gets dark, so that our departure won't attract attention. We want to reach Cuyler Harbor on the island by Tuesday daylight, so we'll need all night to get there."

A few moments later a chauffeur brought Mr. Kleveland's black Cadillac up the drive to give Tommy a lift home.

"The Navy isn't granting you much time for this job, is it?" Tommy asked.

Mr. Kleveland shrugged. "I had to pull strings all the way to the Pentagon to get even a three-day landing permit. They have targets all over the place for air-to-ground missile practice, both night and day. So we've got to locate the galleon, the chart and Cabrillo's bones by Thursday sundown—or wait at least sixty days for another chance."

As Tommy waved good-by from the limousine, he caught sight of Bonilla and Gerlock standing in the window of a second-floor bedroom, earnestly engaged in conversation as they watched the Kleveland car glide off down the drive.

"That QSL card must have shaken them up plenty," Tommy thought gloomily. "It's the worst thing that could have happened. They're forewarned about my suspicions now."

Immediately upon arriving at his home at 2910 Mission View Road, on the Riviera hillside overlooking Santa Bonita, Tommy made a beeline for the double garage, where a second story room housed Amateur Radio station K6ATX.

Seeing his beloved radio gear awaiting him under vinyl dustcovers, needing only to switch on the 120-volt AC to get on the air, Tommy was sorely tempted to fire up his two-meter base station and ragchew with his local pals on the Channel Cities Net, especially his favorite YL, or Young Lady, K6OAD, Gina. But that would be a violation of his oath of secrecy to Mr. Kleveland, so Tommy did not even remove the summer dustcovers from his equipment.

He did take advantage of the opportunity to telephone the sheriff, however, and gave Ross Jackson a detailed report of his meeting the two conspirators—if such they were—at the Kleveland luncheon.

"That QSL card showing up almost floored me," Tommy confessed, "but I've got to hand it to Dr. Bonilla—or Lou Weber, if that's his real name. He sure thought up a story to explain that picture of EA7WK in a hurry."

The sheriff said, "I wonder why he bothered to disguise himself to look like the real Dr. Bonilla in the first place?"

"He brought along a scrapbook of newspaper clippings that showed Dr. Bonilla on scientific expeditions all over the world," Tommy explained, "and the pictures resembled his disguise close enough for Mr. Kleveland to accept them as proof of identity."

After a pause, Ross Jackson said, "Did the photocopy of the page in the *St. Regis'* logbook look convincing?"

"Who can say? Impossible to know whether the picture was of a counterfeit or not. But certainly easy enough to fake."

"How do you think things will develop? Any ideas?"

Tommy made himself comfortable on the sofa in one corner of the hamshack.

"Sure, I've got it all figured out. We'll anchor in Cuyler Harbor where Cabrillo anchored. Ed Morin will send his submarine tractor out to Sombrero Rock, and the TV screen will reveal an object of some kind—a rock, or a chunk of wreckage of one kind or another. Gerlock will put on his scuba bottles and swim out there, and when he comes back he'll be bringing a chunk of lead with a map carved on it, which he'll say he found on the wreck of the galleon. Who's to say he's lying?"

"Meaning he's been out to Sombrero Rock previously and planted this fake map on the lead plate?"

"Either that, or he'll smuggle the chart down there in his diving togs."

Ross Jackson said, "There's a good way to find out whether

Gerlock actually found a galleon's hulk or not."

"How's that? I don't expect the television picture to be sharp enough to really tell us anything on shore."

"You're a skin diver," the sheriff reminded Tommy. "Go out to Sombrero Rock with Gerlock."

Tommy's heart leaped, then sank. "I left my scuba gear up in Washington."

"So what? Call Don Duckett at the Diver's Den. He has your measurements. Rent a wet suit and a pair of bottles and a set of weights. When Gerlock hits the surf to swim out to Sombrero Rock, be right alongside him."

Tommy pulled in a long breath, a strange excitement stirring every fiber in his being.

"Ross, you've done it. I mean, I'll do it by golly. As Spud would say, it's a ding-dong doozie-roo of an idea."

"And if anything develops, radio me ship-to-shore tomorrow night. I can fly out in the county helicopter at a moment's notice. San Miguel is part of my jurisdiction, you know."

"Roger-doger," yawned Tommy. "Seventy-three, Ross."

Tommy drifted off to sleep without realizing it. Tomorrow, he knew, would be the longest, most boring day of his life, lying low in his hamshack. But the promise of adventure to come would more than make up for the tedious wait.

CHAPTER SEVEN

DISASTER IN THE DARK

Tommy's nerves were keyed to a high pitch of excitement by the time the Kleveland chauffeur delivered him to the municipal wharf just after dark the following day, Monday.

A full moon painted its bright yellow track across the black waters of the Santa Barbara Channel, and threw into stark relief the rugged coast range mountains rising four thousand feet behind the city.

The wharf's night watchman unlocked a gate to admit Tommy and his two duffle bags to the area that was closed to the general public at nightfall.

One of the duffle bags contained the diving suit, face mask, flippers and scuba bottles that the Diver's Den had sent Tommy by special delivery earlier in the afternoon. The other bag contained his father's eiderdown sleeping bag, some extra clothing, two portable CB radios, which might come in handy for intercom purposes on the expedition, and a thirty-five-millimeter camera in a watertight housing for underwater work.

Reaching the head of the ramp that led down to the wharf's main loading float twenty feet below, Tommy made out the square, unlovely contours of the Union Oil Company's crane barge *Triton IV*. She was blacked out save for red and green running lights and a white signal lamp atop her lofty crane.

As he started down the cleated ramp, Tommy was challenged by someone on the forward deck whistling the Morse letters Q-R-Z, which translated, in this instance, to "Who goes there?"

"Alfa Tango X-ray," Tommy responded with the phonetics of his ham call, for he recognized the lookout as cub reporter Spud Kleveland.

Spud came back with four dots followed by two dots, "HI," the universal greeting whenever two radio hams met.

Chester Kleveland, dressed in a quilted Navy jacket, blue jeans and sneakers, was waiting at the foot of the ramp with a beefy-shouldered giant in an oilskin slicker.

"Tommy," the newspaperman said, "I believe you know Captain George Tucker, skipper of the *Triton IV*. This is our last passenger, skipper, so we can get under way whenever you say."

Tommy and Captain Tucker, who had known each other for years, exchanged handshakes.

"Two duffle bags?" the captain chided Tommy. "My barge has only been chartered for three days. You must be expecting a round-the-world cruise!"

Tommy laughed but made no comment. He did not want to adver-tise the fact, just yet, that he was bringing scuba diving gear and two transistorized transceivers on board.

The *Triton IV* was the ugly duckling of Santa Bonita harbor, a workhorse designed for tidelands offshore oil well drilling. She was square of prow and stern, although she was self-propelled. Her fore and after decks were crowded with hoisting machinery. Two-thirds of her length was covered with a deckhouse, which, had it not been for the girders of her crane boom and mast, would have made the *Triton IV* look like Noah's Ark.

Chester Kleveland had chartered the crane barge for two reasons—because a crane or derrick of some kind was needed to hoist the TV tractor overboard, and because her shallow draft would enable her to navigate through the reef outside Cuyler Harbor on San Miguel Island.

Normally, Captain Tucker would have a crew of five aboard, but owing to the secret nature of this three-day charter, the tractor's operator Ed Morin would double as chief engineer for the fifty-mile voyage, and the guests would have to do their own cooking.

Tommy Rockford, who had gone cruising on the *Triton IV* several times in the past as a guest of the skipper's, knew that the rear half of the deckhouse was given over to a messroom, galley and head, while the forward half was divided into bunkrooms and washroom facilities for a maximum crew of ten men. A compartment known as "Stateroom A" was more luxuriously furnished than the others, and served Captain Tucker as his private quarters, since drilling jobs often kept the barge at sea for months at a time.

"I've assigned Dr. Bonilla and Mr. Gerlock to my cabin," Captain Tucker informed Tommy. "They've already turned in. I understand neither of them are very good sailors and we're probably in for some pretty choppy water between here and San Miguel tonight. You'll share Bunkroom Two with Spud; Mr. Kleveland and I will be in Bunkroom One."

Tommy walked along the narrow starboard deck to the door marked "2," designating his quarters for the voyage. He was glad to get his duffle bags stowed away without having Dr. Bonilla or Gerlock discover they were aboard.

"Ed Morin's with us, sir?" Tommy asked the skipper.

"He's below waiting for the telegraph bell to signal him to start engines," Captain Tucker explained. "After we get under way you'll probably find him aft, making sure his RUM is lashed down securely in case of rough weather."

"Rum?" Tommy repeated. "Don't tell me the *Triton IV* has gone into the rum-running business—with a top speed of five knots with a tail wind!"

"No," laughed the skipper, who was used to having fun poked at his crane barge. "RUM is what the Navy calls the underwater tractor that's going to haul the television gimmick for us."

After the captain and Mr. Kleveland had left for the wheelhouse, Spud appeared in the bunkroom doorway.

"When are we going to let Dad know we're investigating Dr. Bonilla and maybe Gerlock?" the boy whispered.

"I asked Ross about that," Tommy replied, "and the sheriff said it would just upset your father if we broke the news of our suspicions prematurely. So for the time being, keep your eyes open and your mouth closed, Spud."

Spud chuckled. "Even if we don't wind up with Cabrillo's bones, my first big newspaper scoop will be a ding-dong doozie-roo."

"Cast off the bow line!" Captain Tucker bawled through his megaphone.

"Aye aye, sir!" shouted Spud in ancient mariner fashion, and scuttled outside.

Tommy headed for the afterdeck, feeling the vibration of the *Triton IV's* mighty diesels as they fed power to the twin screws. The barnacle-crusted pilings alongside gave the illusion of moving away from them while the barge stood motionless.

Then the wharf retreated astern, and the lights of Santa Bonita formed a lovely, twinkling pattern at the base of the Santa Ynez Mountains. Surf made its lonely booming sound along the palm-bordered waterfront of the resort city. Once clear of the concrete breakwater that enclosed the yacht basin, the *Triton IV* swung her square prow on a westerly bearing of 265° to begin her laboring journey against headwinds in the direction of San Miguel Island, duplicating the voyage Cabrillo's ungainly caravels had made four centuries earlier.

A whistle buoy off the port beam wailed in farewell, putting a shiver down Tommy's spine in spite of the all-wool hooded sweatshirt he was wearing to combat the night's chill. He was an imaginative fellow, and the buoy's shriek sounded like the strangled cry of some Spanish sailor who had been lost when the *St. Regis* went down off Sombrero Rock.

This time tomorrow he might have found some of those mariners' skeletons in the spectral hull of the sunken galleon...But what was he saying? Of course they would find no sunken galleon—that was a figment of Dr. Bonilla's criminal imagination!

The afterdeck of the barge was jammed with winch drums, capstans and other heavy-duty marine equipment. Reaching the stern rail as the *Triton IV* hit its stride of five knots, Tommy noticed for the first time that they were towing a sleek motor launch, which he recognized as the *Galloping Goose,* belonging to his friend Ed Morin. Tommy had skimmed many a mile on water skis behind Ed at the helm of the old *Goose.*

The glowing red eye of a cigarette appeared in a canopied well marking a companionway belowdecks, and Ed Morin stepped out into the moonlight, smelling of the engine room. He was a stockily built man in his early forties with a neat haircut and a perpetual five-o'clock shadow blueing his cheeks and jaws.

A graduate electronics engineer, Ed had been largely responsible for Tommy's choosing the same career. As W6SNI, Ed Morin was one of the first American hams to bounce Amateur Radio signals off the moon and, later, off the *Echo I* satellite balloon. Ed had also been Tommy's diving instructor in more recent years.

"Thought you were mountain climbing up north," W6SNI said in greeting. "Kleveland isn't very choosy who he takes on his cruises, is he?"

"Seeing that you're chief engineer, I'd say he had scraped under the bottom of the barrel," K6ATX quipped. "Hey, how come you brought the *Goose* along? Will we be water skiing?"

Ed grinned, flipping his cigarette over the side. "As soon as I've accomplished my mission with the RUM tractor," he said, "I'll be heading home in the *Goose*. I won't be needed for the shore part of this project, whatever it may be."

If Ed was fishing for information, he got none.

"Is this mysterious object the RUM?" Tommy asked, pointing to a tarpaulin-covered machine alongside them. Getting Ed's nod, Tommy went on, "What's the scoop on it? I don't believe I've ever seen one."

Ed Morin started unlashing the tarp. "Not many people have," he said. "It's a Navy invention, released for use by salvage outfits and oil companies and the like. I find it very handy as a vehicle for my submarine television camera."

When he removed the tarpaulin, Tommy Rockford had his first close-up look—indeed, his only look to date—at the "RUM."

At first glance it reminded him of a cross between a medium-sized bulldozer and a small army tank, with cleated metal tracks like a tractor, rather than wheels, for propulsion. On top of the machine was an object resembling a six-foot-diameter bass drum, which he soon discovered was a spool of heavy black coaxial cable.

"Why do you call it a RUM?" Tommy wanted to know.

"Navy abbreviation for 'Remote Underwater Manipulator,' " responded Ed. "It began with the hull and track assembly of an Ontos tank, which is the self-propelled cannon used by the Marines. The Navy added a boom-mounted mechanical arm and a television observation system. The whole thing's operated by remote control, through the coax cable, from ship or shore."

On the front end of the RUM was a massive metal arm with a clawlike "hand" that could be opened and closed at the will of the operator. It had a pivoting elbow and a shoulder that could pivot and rotate at the same time. When extended, Ed explained, the RUM's arm had a fifteen-foot reach. At the moment, for shipping, the manipulator was lashed in a retracted position, reminding Tommy of a dentist's drill folded in its rack.

"This iron claw is just as maneuverable as my own right hand," Ed went on to say. "I can move it up or down, right or left, all by push-button control. I think I could run this gadget a mile away from shore, out of sight on the bottom of the ocean, and pick up an egg without cracking the shell. And for heavy-duty lifting below the sea, the RUM can handle anything."

Mounted alongside the cable-wound drum was a watertight housing with a monstrous white eye peering behind a porthole. In the moonlight it gave the RUM the look of a mechanical Cyclops.

"This is your submarine floodlight, I take it?" Tommy asked.

"Right. And the smaller cylinder on the other side houses the TV camera's vidicon tube—so sensitive I can't open the iris in daylight without burning it out."

Trying to sound intelligent, Tommy commented, "I wouldn't think a TV camera would be much good on a muddy bottom, with the floodlight picking up the smudge."

"Out where we're going," Ed Morin gave away his first hint that he knew the goal of their secret expedition, "the Coast and Geodetic Survey charts show clean white sand and rock bottom. I'm more concerned about the camera's being blinded by bladder kelp than about the RUM's kicking up a smudge."

"What's the range of this contraption?"

"Only the limit of your cable. This one carries six thousand feet—over a mile. The Navy's explored down to twenty thousand feet with no mechanical difficulties."

The next few minutes were occupied in restoring the tarp cover in place and lashing it down.

Then Tommy said suddenly, "Ed, after your TV camera has found what it's expected to find—if it finds anything at all—Kurt Gerlock will make the dive to examine it, won't he?"

Ed parried the leading question cagily.

"Classified information, kid. I've been sworn to secrecy."

Tommy grinned. "All right, let me put it this way. When he makes the dive, will he be alone?"

"N-No," Ed said, "I'll be diving with him. Too dangerous to send a man down alone."

Tommy nodded. "I see. Ed, I want you to do me a tremendous favor. I want to make that dive with Gerlock instead of you. I can't tell you why, not just yet, but it's terribly important."

Ed Morin's eyes burned into his.

"It'll be a dangerous dive, Tommy. I don't think I ought to allow you to take my risks." He paused, as if trying to reach a decision. "But I will. For the reason that Ross Jackson called me up last night and asked me to."

With which Ed Morin turned and disappeared down the engine-room companionway out of sight.

"I wonder," Tommy mused as he started working his way across the crowded afterdeck toward the starboard walkway leading to his bunkroom, "if the danger Ed had in mind was rip currents—or Kurt Gerlock as a diving companion...?"

That riddle was working on Tommy's mind, occupying his attention, when he entered the jet-black shadow of the deckhouse and started working his way forward. The clumsy barge was bucking fairly heavy seas, and the iron-plated deck made footing precarious.

At the point where he now found himself, opposite the doorway of the messroom and galley, there was no outer railing to protect him from going overboard if he made a misstep on the slippery deck.

He was groping his way past the messroom doorway when it came—disaster out of the dark, and without warning.

The back of his head seemed to explode in a blaze of red fireworks. He was only vaguely aware of sprawling face-down on the deck; and then the starboard side of the barge seemed to dip, sliding him toward the edge as the *Triton IV* wallowed in a green valley of salt water.

Did something shove him in the ribs, at the instant he was catapulted over the edge into empty blackness? The hissing, froth-flecked waters of the Channel seemed to reach up to pluck his hurtling body out of space, and the impact of hitting the icy brine seemed almost as hard as dropping on a concrete pavement.

Then a salty surge engulfed Tommy Rockford, the bitter coldness of the seawater serving to clear his brain momentarily.

Had he accidentally banged his head on some unseen obstruction up there—or had he been slugged from behind and dumped overboard by some unknown human hand to drown?

CHAPTER EIGHT

CABRILLO'S DESERT ISLAND

U p from black, unplumbed depths of brine rose Tommy Rockford's limply helpless body. As consciousness returned, he felt himself being buffeted by the angry churn of the *Triton IV*'s twin propellers, like ice cream in a milk shake mixer.

Then he broke surface in a smother of foam, and knew he was but moments away from death.

Mere seconds ago, he had been heading along the barge deck toward his cabin; now he was trapped in frigid waters, his throat too paralyzed from shock for him to shout for help, even if anyone aboard the lumbering scow could have heard his cries.

Instinct took over for Tommy Rockford now, and his life-long swimming experience. He was not weighted down with heavy clothing, so he could stay afloat. His immediate fear was of being sucked into the *Triton IV*'s spinning screw blades and being chopped to shark bait.

But he had surfaced in time. The *Triton IV* was past now, the gliding wall of planks and rivets giving way to a glimpse of a bobbing horizon and the low hills of Santa Cruz Island. That shoreline was at least fifteen miles away. He would perish from exposure long before he could swim that awful distance.

Something black and sinuous, like a huge snake, cut across the moon and stars to slap the water inches from Tommy's head, with a noise like a rifle shot at close range. It was the bight of the towline that led from the barge to the *Galloping Goose,* Ed Morin's speedboat.

New hope came to Tommy's flagging spirit in that instant. Once again instinct took over, as it had made him inflate his lungs during his brief hurtle toward the waves a few moments before.

With the desperation only the doomed can know, Tommy hooked both elbows over the inch-thick hawser. The next instant he was being physically jerked out of the water when the towline yanked taut, suspending him momentarily above a heaving, lather-flecked trough of sea between foaming wave crests.

Then he was dropping into the yawning valley of phosphorescence from the *Triton IV*'s wake, hitting the water with a force that seemed as if it would break every bone in his body. But the desperate youth did not loose his grip, sick and faint as he was, for in that moment he first realized he had a fighting, outside chance for survival.

There was no use shouting for help. No ear aboard the barge could hear him above the whine of a forty-mile wind in the crane rigging, above the ceaseless slap of waves assaulting the square prow, above the throbbing roar of the big diesels.

If anyone was watching from the barge, it would be the person who had slugged him and rolled his body over the edge—for Tommy would never believe his fall had been accidental. And that person would hardly toss him a cork ring or a lifejacket. It was up to him to save himself.

He would die of exposure within a short while if he let go his grip on the towline. Yet his body could not endure many more spankings on the passing wave tops as the tow rope alternately sagged and snapped taut.

Tommy began working his way hand over hand along the tarred hawser, underwater one moment, above the waves the next. He knew he would not have the strength to climb the hawser to the deck of the barge, twenty feet above; but the *Galloping Goose*'s hull was low to the water, and its sleek teakwood length had various rails and cleats and other fixtures to afford handholds.

He had worked his way to within ten feet of the bouncing prow of the *Galloping Goose* when the launch yawed suddenly and jerked the rope from the grasp of Tommy's numbed and bleeding hands.

Horror was in him as he went under. "Only one chance now," he told himself. "Grab launch or I'm finished..." They wouldn't even know he had fallen overboard, most likely, until they found his bunk hadn't been slept in next morning.

The launch was already halfway past him when he surfaced

alongside. He felt his flailing hands slide off the varnished fiberglass surface of the hull.

Then, dimly seen in the moonlight, Tommy made out the doughnut-shaped outline of a heavy braided bumper made of hemp that hung from the chrome handrailing amidships.

Tommy lunged at the passing bumper with both arms. He sank fingers bent like iron spikes into the knotted cordage. His grip was good and the knowledge that his life literally hung in the balance gave him strength to counteract the numbing cold and the aftermath of shock from whatever blow had caused him to tumble off the *Triton IV* in the first place.

His head was clearer now, so that he could let his intelligence, rather than instinct alone, take control. When the next wave lifted him above the bumper, Tommy let go with his right hand and grabbed the starboard rail.

He clung there a moment, his hips and legs still dragging in the ocean, while he sucked air into his lungs in great, sobbing gusts. Then, feeling the coldness of the water numbing his legs and creeping in a slow paralysis up his spine, Tommy flexed his powerful arm muscles to chin himself up, up and over the mahogany gunwale. Then he was somersaulting head over heels to the safety of the duct boards on the cockpit decking.

The *Galloping Goose* was bobbing like its namesake at the end of its flailing leash, but Tommy didn't mind. He was safe now. Nothing else mattered.

For several minutes he lay there, getting over his dizziness and nausea. He realized he had to get out of the cold wind soon, or risk catching pneumonia.

Lifting the cushioned seat of one of the cockpit benches, Tommy pulled a lifejacket from the compartment beneath. Then he groped forward on all fours, reached for the brass knob of the launch cabin— and found it unlocked.

A moment later he was inside the snug cabin, out of the biting wind. From long acquaintance with Ed Morin's launch, he knew his way around in the dark.

In case his unknown attacker might be watching from the deck of the crane barge, Tommy drew curtains over the cabin ports and sloping windshield before turning on a binnacle light. Under no circumstances could he let it be known that he had snagged a ride on the trailing *Goose.*

His first move was to strip out of his drenched clothing and shoes. From a locker he found a bedraggled pair of Navy dungaree pants and one of Ed's YMCA sweatshirts with a hood.

The dry clothing began to restore warmth to Tommy's body. He groped forward into the lavatory compartment and, after making sure the porthole was shielded with a draw curtain, snapped on a light above the mirror. The glass revealed an ugly, bleeding lump on the side of his skull above his left ear, where an object of some kind had struck him as he was passing the *Triton IV*'s galley.

Assuming that he hadn't stumbled and knocked himself out, who would want to attack him? It hardly seemed reasonable that Dr. Bonilla, even if he was the notorious swindler Lou Weber, would want Tommy murdered. After all, they had no way of knowing that he suspected a conspiracy to defraud Mr. Kleveland—unless the unfortunate discovery of the Spanish QSL card had panicked them.

Tommy opened a first-aid kit he found in the wall cabinet and swabbed the welt on his scalp with mercurochrome, dusted it with antiseptic powder and applied an adhesive bandage.

"The heck of it is," Tommy groaned with frustration, "I may never find out what happened tonight. But one thing sure, I can watch my step from here on out."

Back in the cabin of the *Galloping Goose,* Tommy looked over Ed Morin's marine electronic gear—sonar, fathometer, radar, radio compass and radio telephone. Ed's launch was equipped with almost as much gear as the *Queen Mary.*

The fact that the barge had not altered speed or course told Tommy that his absence had not yet been noted by anyone on board.

Morin's high-powered binoculars hung from a spoke of the helm at his side. Removing them from their case, Tommy turned off the binnacle light, drew back the windshield curtain, and focused the glasses on the *Triton IV*'s pilot house some two hundred feet ahead.

He could see Captain Tucker and Chester Kleveland standing there, silhouetted by the binnacle lamp in the wheelhouse. It would be a simple matter to switch on the powerful spotlight of the *Galloping Goose* and gain their attention. But did he want to be taken back aboard the barge just yet?

Going outside, Tommy turned the binoculars toward the coast, along which the fifty-mile stretch of Santa Barbara Channel lay in a due northerly direction.

He could see a cluster of lights marking the university campus, which told him they were now about seven miles west of Santa Bonita. The binoculars picked up a colorful cartoon comedy flickering on the giant movie screen of the drive-in theater at Goleta, the college town directly off the starboard beam. He saw the silvery shape of a 727 jet taking off for San Francisco, its wing lights flashing.

"I've got to let the skipper know I'm okay before Spud discovers my bunk isn't occupied," Tommy decided, and ducked back into the closed cabin of the launch.

He turned on Ed's marine transceiver and switched to Channel three—a ship-to-ship frequency used mainly by commercial fishermen—and picked up the push-to-talk microphone.

"Calling Barge *Triton IV,* Calling Barge *Triton IV,* this is the launch *Galloping Goose* calling. Do you read me?"

The only sound Tommy heard issuing from the speaker on that frequency was a tuna clipper off Acapulco exchanging weather reports with another fisherman near the Galapagos Islands.

Which of the frequencies did Captain Tucker monitor on board the barge? Tommy reviewed the other four crystal positions on Ed's radio. Channel One, he knew, was the ship-to-shore frequency he would be using to contact Sheriff Ross Jackson tomorrow. Channels Two and Four were distress slots only, monitored twenty-four hours a day by the Coast Guard. That left Channel Five for ship-to-ship traffic, and was probably the one Captain Tucker kept tuned in on the *Triton IV.*

Tommy repeated his call on Channel Five. He was answered immediately by Captain Tucker's startled voice: "QRZ the launch calling Barge *Triton IV*? Over."

"This is the *Galloping Goose* calling and by. Do you read?"

There was a moment's silence. Through the glasses, Tommy could see Captain Tucker and Mr. Kleveland in consulation, peering back through the wheelhouse window in his direction.

"Is this some weirdo's idea of a joke?" Captain Tucker growled into his mike. "I've got the *Galloping Goose* under tow."

"Maybe it's a stowaway!" came Mr. Kleveland's excited cry off-mike. "Some reporter from a Los Angeles newspaper may have sneaked aboard!"

"Repeat name of launch, please?" Captain Tucker said. "Over."

Tommy stifled a chuckle. "The *Galloping Goose,* sir. This is K6ATX. There are no stowaways aboard, Mr. Kleveland."

Through the binoculars, Tommy saw Chester Kleveland snatch the microphone from Captain Tucker.

"Tommy! What are you doing aboard the *Galloping Goose*?"

K6ATX replied sheepishly, "I-I fell overboard, sir."

"*Fell overboard!*" It was the captain again. "How? When?"

"Fifteen minutes ago, sir. I grabbed the towline and crawled aboard the launch. I'm perfectly okay sir—dry clothing and everything. I just wanted to let you know why I wouldn't be in my bunk in the morning."

Captain Tucker's voice held a somber note of worry as he came back, "Are you sure you're okay? How in thunder could a husky sailor like you fall off a lousy barge?"

"*I only wish I knew,*" thought Tommy. Aloud, he reassured the men in the wheelhouse of the *Triton IV*: "I'm fit as a fiddle, sir. No need to stop and haul me aboard the barge. I'll bunk here tonight and see you all in the morning, okay?"

Tucker and Kleveland went into another conference. Finally Tucker said, "If you're positive you're safe and comfortable, Tommy, we won't take you aboard now. It would be a pretty slow job to accomplish in this rough sea, and I've got to hit the Devil's Jaw inlet to Cuyler Harbor at full high tide or risk anchoring outside all morning."

Kleveland added, "We've only got tomorrow and Wednesday and Thursday to operate on the Island, Tommy, so every minute counts. Are you sure you're all right?"

Tommy radioed back, "A hundred percent, sir. I-I'd appreciate it if you didn't tell anyone aboard about this. It's pretty embarrassing."

"We won't," Captain Tucker promised. "And don't apologize. Just thank God you didn't drown. It was a miracle you escaped."

Tommy said, "Good night. Launch *Galloping Goose* signing clear, but monitoring the frequency all night in case you need to call me for any reason."

"Roger," acknowledged Captain Tucker, and set down his microphone.

Suddenly overpowered with weariness as the reaction of his recent ordeal in the water made itself felt on his nervous system, Tommy crawled into one of the *Galloping Goose's* four bunks, pulled a Navy blanket up around his ears, and tried to relax.

No religious fanatic, Tommy had been brought up with a solid, realistic faith in his Creator, and his last conscious thought on the brink of sleep was a prayer of thanksgiving to Him: "Thanks a lot, God. I know I wouldn't have made it tonight if You hadn't given me a helping hand when I needed it so badly. Thanks."

A foggy, gray dawn was breaking over the Channel Islands when the ship-to-ship radio woke Tommy out of his drugged sleep:

"Rise and shine, Tommy! I'm here to take you aboard the barge before anybody else is up and around. I'll need a lookout up for'd when we start nosing through the Devil's Jaw into the harbor, and you're elected."

Tommy scrambled topside to find a fog-hazed sun poised over the chaparral-covered hills of Santa Rosa Island immediately east of San Miguel Island. The crane barge was wallowing in the groundswells off the northern coast of San Miguel, which loomed like a gray whaleback, sand-streaked and forbidding, off their port beam.

It was biting cold for a July morning. Twenty-five miles to the north, across the Channel, was the stubby lighthouse at Point Concepcion, where California turned the corner to form an elbow of land which shielded the Channel from the full brunt of winter gales and summer surf.

Captain Tucker was at the controls of a small windlass near the *Triton IV*'s stern, reeling in the *Galloping Goose*'s towline. Tommy made his way to the forepeak and caught the dangling rope ladder hanging from the boxlike stern of the barge. Moments later he was scrambling to the deck to shake Captain Tucker's hand, and the launch was permitted to slack off astern.

"Nobody's up yet to witness my disgrace?" Tommy asked sheepishly.

"I won't blast the getting-up whistle until we're safe inside the Devil's Jaw," the barge captain said. "Say, that's a nasty lump on your noggin, son. What happened last night?"

Tommy pointed to the narrow walkway between the deckhouse and the starboard railing. "Ed had been showing me the RUM tractor here, and I was on my way to my bunk when I must have slipped. Anyway, the next I knew I was dunked. If I hadn't latched onto the towline, the barracudas would have had me for breakfast by now."

Heading for the front of the barge where he would stand lookout during the difficult passage of the Devil's Jaw inlet into the harbor, Tommy had a good long look at the area near the open doorway of the messroom. He satisfied himself on one point: There was no projecting obstacle into which he could have accidentally cracked his head in the dark.

The only other explanation for the blow on his skull was that some object, like a bucket or a tool, had rolled off the upper decking of the deckhouse and struck him just as he was passing underneath. Tommy rejected that as preposterous.

Up forward, Tommy had his first close-up view of San Miguel Island in several years. From previous visits he knew the uninhabited island was roughly triangular in shape, some eight miles long from east to west, and from two to five miles in width.

Over four hundred years ago, when Cabrillo had anchored in this cove, now called Cuyler Harbor after the US engineer who had surveyed it, San Miguel had been heavily populated with Stone Age aborigines, and was covered with chaparral and wind-stunted trees.

But today, San Miguel presented a scene of utter desolation. A few weatherbeaten barns and fences on a plateau some six hundred feet above the beach marked the abandoned sheep ranch which had been here during the 1930s; behind that shelf an unnamed sand ridge loomed to a height of eight hundred feet.

Cabrillo's anchorage was guarded by a reef of jagged rocks with sixty-acre Prince Island on one side and a fang of stone called Sombrero Rock, from its resemblance to a Mexican hat, on the other.

The sight of Sombrero Rock had a new meaning to Tommy Rockford this chill summer morning. Under the boiling surf at its foot, Kurt Gerlock claimed, they would find a phantom Spanish galleon! Before the day was over they would know if Gerlock was lying.

CHAPTER NINE

GHOSTS OF SAN MIGUEL

T he Devil's Jaw was fanged with submerged rocks at high tide, with barely room enough for a barge as wide as the *Triton IV* to navigate safely. Even with diesel power, the passage of the narrow inlet was a touch-and-go thing; yet the helmeted and breastplated mariners of Cabrillo's day had accomplished it with sail-propelled caravels.

With Tommy in the prow keeping watch for shoals which the helmsman in the wheelhouse could not see because of the barge's overhang, the *Triton IV* steered precariously through the white water marking the Devil's Jaw. Only Captain Tucker was aware that the keel scraped bottom more than once. The cove itself ranged in depth from one to seven fathoms, but it was dotted with rocks and fouled with brown patches of kelp, making it altogether an undesirable anchorage.

Not until he had four anchors out, bow and stern, in the lee of the peninsula which the maps called Harris Point, did Tucker switch off his engines and give a mighty blast on the *Triton*'s air-powered foghorn to wake his five sleeping passengers.

Ed Morin was the first on deck, and the only person Tommy informed about his mishap of the night before—which he could not avoid, inasmuch as Ed recognized Tommy's change of costume as having come from the *Galloping Goose*'s locker.

Before they could discuss Tommy's misadventure, Kurt Gerlock and Dr. Bonilla emerged from Stateroom A, the captain's cabin. If either of them had cause to be surprised at finding Tommy Rockford on board safe and sound this morning, he masked it well.

Shortly afterward Mr. Kleveland and Spud, the latter feverishly jotting down notes for a future newspaper article, joined the others on deck. In the excitement of seeing Cabrillo's mysterious island at close range, no one seemed to notice the tape on Tommy's skull.

Viewed from the anchored barge, a stone's throw from the narrow shingled beach, San Miguel seemed as desolate and deserted as any desert island of fiction. Long since vanished were the conical reed huts of the original Canaliño Indians who had lived here when Cabrillo arrived in 1542. The only visible indication that man had ever set foot on San Miguel prior to this morning was a squat, flat-roofed concrete-walled hut some fifty feet above high-tide mark.

A row of toredo-eaten piling stumps indicated where a landing dock had been when the Navy maintained a radar station here. On the beach above it was a weatherbeaten sign reading

VISITORS ARE WARNED THAT SAN MIGUEL
ISLAND AND ADJACENT WATERS ARE OFF
LIMITS ON ACCOUNT OF MISSILE AND
BOMBING PRACTICE WITHOUT NOTICE.
US NAVY

"That concrete blockhouse over there," Mr. Kleveland explained to Bonilla and Gerlock, "was part of the Navy installation here after a Japanese submarine shelled the coast near here in 1942. There is a white circle and cross painted on the roof—I guess you know what that means."

Spud looked up from his note-taking. "I don't, Dad."

"It means that radar hut has been marked as a target when the Point Arguello Missile Facility starts its air-to-ground bombing runs next Friday. That's why we have to get our work done and clear out. That blockhouse will be blown to atoms before the weekend is over, along with other targets on the island."

Ed Morin was busy studying the concrete hut through his glasses. It had one rusty iron door, facing west, and a narrow, slotlike observation window facing the harbor.

"Mr. Kleveland," Morin inquired, "would there be any objection to my setting up my RUM controls and television console in that radar shack? I'd much rather work on land than aboard the barge, the way these groundswells are running."

Mr. Kleveland shrugged. "Inasmuch as the Navy plans to bomb the hut out of existence in a few days anyway, I don't imagine they'd object to your getting your electronic gear in out of the weather, Ed."

Tommy and Spud, as the younger members of the expedition, could forget about dignity and made no bones about their impatience to get ashore. Captain Tucker, however, insisted that everyone pitch in and help prepare breakfast before work began.

With everyone so excited about the prospect of getting ashore and putting the submarine tractor to work exploring the ocean bottom at the base of Sombrero Rock, there was no difficulty in getting volunteers to start work in the galley.

Dr. Bonilla seated himself at the mess table nearest the open doorway—through which Tommy believed an assailant had clubbed him down the night before—and kept staring at the steep slope of the island's north wall as if he could almost picture the ghosts of Cabrillo's crew stalking the sand and rocks.

Chester Kleveland, who probably knew as much about the history of the Channel islands as any layman in California, politely asked his Spanish guest to tell something about the historical background of this sinister and forbidding spot.

Dr. Bonilla, sipping coffee with relish, waved an arm to take in the scene roundabout.

"Right here in this harbor where Cabrillo anchored his ships, *La Victoria* and *San Salvador,* he had the bad luck to fall and break a shoulder. This was in the autumn of 1542.

"But the King of Spain had commissioned him to explore the west coast of the New World, so Cabrillo took his little ships as far north as perhaps San Francisco Bay, which he overlooked entirely in the fog. All this time, Cabrillo's broken shoulder was developing gangrene.

"Winter storms finally drove Cabrillo's ships back down the coast and around Point Concepcion," Dr. Bonilla went on, sounding almost as if he were reciting something memorized out of a history textbook— which in Tommy's private opinion was probably what he was actually doing.

"Thus he found himself back to this very spot on the Isle of Possession—his name for San Miguel—anchoring here in this harbor

66

where our barge is anchored today."

When Dr. Bonilla paused as if to ransack his memory, Spud prompted him with "The gangrene eventually caused his death, didn't it?"

Dr. Bonilla reached up to adjust the plastic patch over his left eyesocket. "I can quote you his pilot's entry in the logbook word for word, Señor Spud. Bartolme Ferrello was the pilot's name, and this is exactly what he wrote—the original log is in my museum in Seville:

Passing the winter on the Island of La Posesion, on the third of the month of January 1543, Juan Rodriguez Cabrillo, captain of said ships, departed from this life, as the result of a fall which he suffered on said Island when they were there before, from which he broke an arm near the shoulder. He left as Captain the chief pilot, Bartolme Ferrello. He named the island 'Juan Rodriguez,' although the Indians called it Ciquimuymu.

"Unfortunately for generations of historians to follow, Ferrello made no record of where Cabrillo was buried, except the lead chart which he took to the King of Spain. And in 1581, when the galleon *St. Regis* visited this island to disinter Cabrillo's bones for return to Spain, it was wrecked. If we are lucky, we may find the wreckage of that galleon before today's sun has set. This is a memorable occasion, gentlemen."

The history lecture appeared to be over, so with a mischievious glint in his eye, Tommy decided to needle the man he was convinced was a faker.

"If we should dig up a skeleton in armor," K6ATX asked, "how could you prove it was Cabrillo's, Doctor?"

Dr. Bonilla smiled patiently. "Having spent most of my life in this field," he said, "there will be certain irrefutable clues for me to examine. For example, the records tell us that Cabrillo was buried in helmet, breastplate and with sword. The archives give us the name of the armorer who did the work, and his hallmark should be on both helmet and breastplate, as well as the mark of the Toledo artisan who forged his sword."

When breakfast was finished, the party went back on deck to find that an eight o'clock sun had dissipated the mists. A thirty-mile wind was bearing in from the northwest, capping the waves on the channel with white and ruffling long scarves of blowsand across San Miguel's hills and gullies.

Sea lions lazed on the surf-drenched rocks at the foot of Sombrero, just outside the harbor entrance. Myriads of wild-fowl—cormorants, gulls and pelicans—nested atop the guano-whitened crown of Sombrero Rock, the descendants, perhaps, of the sea birds that had witnessed the original wreck of the *St. Regis.*

The remaining morning hours were busy ones, with all hands finding plenty of work to do.

Captain Tucker, who had been up all night manning the helm of the *Triton IV,* had one more task before heading for his bunk. The massive crane was swiveled around, a huge chain and hook lowered to the pick-up ring on the RUM tractor, and the submarine explorer was lifted up and swung out over the water as if its three-ton weight were light as a feather.

Tommy and Spud were waiting in the *Galloping Goose* alongside the spot where the RUM would be lowered to the bottom of the harbor. Ed Morin had ridden the tractor off the barge, and when it hung suspended a foot above the water, passed the end of the coaxial control cable to the boys in the launch.

With the cable made fast to a cleat, Tommy sent the launch toward the beach, the cable unwinding from the big drum on the top of the RUM. As soon as the keel of the launch struck the sand, Spud unfastened the cable and hustled up the slope to the abandoned radar hut, some fifty feet above the water mark.

Not until then did Ed Morin swing back up the rope ladder to the deck of the *Triton IV* and signal Captain Tucker to lower the RUM into the water. It sank from sight in a roil of bubbles, and when the cable slacked off to indicate that it had touched bottom, a bit of juggling by the boom of the crane freed the hook from its ring.

Tommy and Spud returned to the barge to pick up a gasoline-powered electric generator mounted on a rubber-tired trailer, which Captain Tucker's crane lowered into the launch. This portable generator would provide the power for the RUM and the television equipment on shore.

Several shuttle trips were necessary between beach and barge before Ed Morin's remote control equipment was ashore and safely stowed inside the concrete-walled radar hut. While all this was going on, Dr. Bonilla and Kurt Gerlock remained on board the barge to clean up the galley after breakfast.

With all his equipment on hand at the concrete blockhouse on shore, Ed Morin went to work with Tommy as his assistant, setting up the remote control station for the underwater exploration to come.

The black, snake-like thread of the coaxial cable that led off into the waters of the harbor to the submerged tractor was now connected to the console. Other heavy-duty power cables led through a ventilator in the south wall of the radar hut and connected to the gasoline generator the boys had rolled ashore and positioned beside the rear of the hut.

Mr. Kleveland's principal activity was shooting photos with his press camera for future use in the *News-Star,* recording all steps in the setting up of the RUM control station.

The TV monitoring screens, four in number, were located above the control panel with its bewildering array of dials, knobs, meters, toggle switches and push-buttons. With the single exception of Tommy, whose knowledge of electronics was extensive for a teenager, the electronic "brain" was too complicated for a layman's comprehension.

Around eleven o'clock, three hours after the first shore party had landed on the beach, Ed Morin went out behind and cranked up the portable generator.

"Stand by, everyone, and we'll see what happens when I warm up the tubes," Ed Morin announced. "I think we're about ready to go."

Excitement flushed every face as the group crowded into the concrete blockhouse, watching with absorbed fascination as Ed Morin's deft, sensitive fingers began playing over his instrument panel as a concert pianist might run arpeggios on a grand-piano keyboard.

The only person missing was Captain Tucker, who was taking a well-deserved sleep aboard the *Triton IV;* but he was no stranger to the RUM's operations and underwater television work, which were in everyday use by the oil companies drilling wells under California's offshore tidelands.

Kurt Gerlock's fixed, jack-o'-lantern grin at least seemed to have a meaning, as he stood behind Ed Morin, his eyes fixed on the main ten-inch monitor screen of the TV receiver.

Tommy, Spud and Mr. Kleveland were arrayed close behind, watching meter needles start dancing as Ed fed power to various transformers and capacitors. Inside the complex-looking cabinet, myriads of electronic devices were heating up to operating temperatures, sending "green worms" crawling weirdly across the calibrated faces of Ed's oscilloscopes.

"Out there in the harbor, twenty-odd feet under the keel of the *Triton IV,* our TV camera and the dozen or so electric motors on the RUM are also warming up for action," Ed explained. "The coax cable is its lifeline. Through it goes the high-voltage current from our generating plant, and the coded impulses by which I make the tractor do my bidding."

A gasp interrupted the hushed stillness inside the radar shack as the TV screen suddenly came aglow. Raster lines raced across the picture tubes. Ed Morin made deft adjustments for brightness, vertical and horizontal sweep and focus, as casually as if he were adjusting a home TV set.

And then, as the spectators watched in breath-held suspense, they saw a school of fish float eerily across the TV screen, then dart away as Ed Morin snapped a switch to swing the powerful mercury-vapor underwater searchlight beam in their direction.

This was what the RUM's cyclopean eye was seeing, out there in the bay a hundred feet from shore.

"Now let's point our camera lens straight up and see what we can see," Morin suggested, pushing a series of buttons to activate tiny motors out on the submerged TV camera.

The camera tilted slowly upward, the screen revealing a patch of ribbon kelp, a floating beer can, then a blurred diagonal shadow of what appeared to be a tree leaning at a 45° angle from the harbor bottom. The true identity of the "tree" became apparent when Morin refocused the camera lens and a series of chain links came into sharp definition.

"The *Triton IV*'s starboard stern anchor chain," explained Ed. "Now, just to demonstrate the flexibility of the RUM equipment for Mr. Gerlock's interest, we'll let the camera follow that chain up to the barge itself."

Link by link the camera seemed to travel up the anchor chain until the barge's propellers and rudder came into view, as seen from directly underneath.

"Now," said Morin, "I'll throw the tractor into forward gear and we'll let the camera travel the whole length of the *Triton's* bottom.

Too bad Captain Tucker isn't here to see this—he could check his hull without having to haul his barge into drydock. I would charge him one hundred dollars an hour for this type of service on a commercial basis."

Toggle switches were snapped by Ed Morin's expert thumb.

To the six pairs of eyes glued to the TV monitor, the illusion was that the barge began to move. Not until the camera had transmitted a clear picture of every inch of the *Triton IV*'s copper-sheathed bottom did Ed Morin turn off the mercury-vapor searchlight to darken the screen.

"The RUM is ready to head for sea, Mr. Gerlock," Ed announced. "I have enough cable to reach a mile off shore. I await your orders."

Gerlock's hands were shaking with excitement as he fished from his wallet the photocopy of the *St. Regis'* logbook and the typewritten translation he had brought back from Spain.

"According to the log of the galleon *St. Regis*," Gerlock said, "she hit a suger-loaf-shaped rock at one hundred twenty degrees and twenty minutes West, thirty-four degrees and three minutes North. On modern charts, those bearings intersect on Cuyler Harbor, so I would say the galleon lies against the north face of Sombrero Rock, in six fathom of water."

Ed Morin eyed Gerlock quizzically. "I didn't know the navigational instruments of the Sixteenth Century were that accurate," he said. "Most of the old Spanish calibrations of latitude and longitude were wide of the mark by as much as a hundred miles."

Tommy smiled inwardly, thinking "You don't know it, Ed, but you touched a raw nerve with that remark. If Gerlock and Lou Weber faked up that map, they didn't take that little detail into account. But what's the difference? There won't be any galleon out there beneath Sombrero Rock anyway."

When neither Bonilla nor Gerlock made any reply to Ed's comment, Morin turned back to his control box.

"Keep your eye on the beach," he said, "for the RUM to come up from the depths and onto dry land. Then it'll head for Sombrero Rock and this show will officially be on the road!"

CHAPTER TEN

UNDERWATER TELEVISION

Now that the great adventure had reached its climactic phase, Spud and his father hurried along the beach so as to be close by when Ed Morin maneuvered the RUM tractor out of the harbor onto the sandspit.

Mr. Kleveland had his press camera and strobe light ready to take sequential pictures of the mechanical monster in action. Spud, as a teenage cub reporter working on the first big story of his infant career, had his notebook poised and waiting.

Dr. Bonilla and Kurt Gerlock remained close by the radar shack, to view what was going on under the sea by means of Ed Morin's television screen, as soon as he turned on the submarine searchlight. Ed had previously explained that he could not use the TV camera in sunlight for fear of causing damage to the supersensitive vidicon tube.

Tommy Rockford, because of his extreme interest in all matters electronic, remained inside the radar hut with Ed.

"Here we go," Ed said, pressing a button to start the RUM's propulsion motor. "I'll steer up and out of the harbor bottom by dead reckoning, Tommy, so keep an eye on the beach about where the Klevelands are waiting and you'll see it surface. As soon as the RUM is submerged in the outer ocean I'll switch on the mercury-vapor lamp and we'll track by TV screen."

"Roger," Tommy responded, and stepped to the open door of the radar shack. Through the tail of his eye he saw Ed advancing the big rheostat marked THROTTLE, to speed up the tractor.

Suddenly, the spectators saw a streak of white appear on the placid surface of the cove, like the feather behind a periscope. Then a black object appeared, which at first glance resembled the dorsal fin of a tiger shark cutting its way through the water. It was the RUM's iron claw.

Suddenly, with a great burst of foam and spray, the underwater TV tractor lurched into view, shedding water as might a giant beast. Sunlight flashed on moving cleats as the RUM crawled like some monstrous crab onto dry land.

The strobe flash on Mr. Kleveland's Graflex camera winked. The white cable drum on the rear of the tractor stopped revolving as Ed halted the RUM in front of the two Klevelands.

Everyone stared fascinated as the RUM, responding in an almost human fashion to Ed Morin's deft manipulation of toggle switches and push-buttons inside the control shack, extended its electro-mechanical arm, reached down to clamp its nippers onto a chunk of driftwood, and while Mr. Kleveland hurriedly snapped pictures, lifted the stick toward the sky as if waving a flag.

"I could snatch the pencil right out of Spud's hand if we had time for horsing around," chuckled W6SNI.

At a signal from Kleveland, indicating that he had all the pictures he wanted at the moment, Ed had the RUM toss the chunk of driftwood aside and fold its mechanical arm.

Internal motors hummed, barely audible to the ear, as the coaxial cable fed them power from the on-shore generator. Then the cleated tracks dug into the sand for footing and the tractor lunged forward at medium speed, clambering effortlessly over driftwood and flotsam.

Spud and his father hooked a ride on the back of the tractor as it topped the sand bar and headed down to the outer beach toward the surf, the slowly revolving drum paying out the coaxial cable in a long black line behind it, the umbilical cord that gave it life and movement.

At the edge of the ocean Morin halted the monster again, to give Mr. Kleveland time to take more pictures and switch to his portable video recorder to record the RUM's plunge into the rolling breakers.

A few adjustments on the operating console, and Ed Morin swung the RUM around heading straight at Sombrero Rock. Another signal from the Klevelands, and Morin advanced the throttle control which sent the RUM out into the shallow water, acting as ponderous as a hippopotamus in an African river.

For a moment the RUM seemed to pause.

"Losing traction in quicksand," Ed Morin muttered, and boosted the power. The RUM extricated its sinking treads from the beach sand and moved forward to breach the first of a series of incoming breakers which seemed to be marshalling strength to hurl back this mechanical invasion of their domain.

Great sheets of spray geysered skyward, bright as quick-silver under the noon sun. Tons of green salt water assaulted the crawling metal monster without appearing to slow it down an iota. Only Morin's fingers moving over the controls let Tommy know that he was finding it necessary to reduce gears and triple power to compensate for the tremendous impact of the surf.

Then, as Tommy watched through his binoculars from the door of the radar hut, he saw the RUM dip under a mammoth green ground-swell. For a moment its elevated cable drum could be glimpsed in the following valley between waves. When the next comber passed over it, the RUM vanished beneath the surface.

Dr. Bonilla and Kurt Gerlock, shouting with excitement, came scrambling up the short slope to reach the radar hut just as Ed Morin switched on the TV section of his control panel.

A red-handled toggle turned on the sun-bright mercury-vapor searchlight. Another toggle, color-coded blue, opened the protective iris shutter of the TV camera lens, which had been kept closed to protect the supersensitive vidicon camera tube from overexposure to sunlight. Still a third switch opened the diaphragm to its full f:1.9 aperture.

"Close the door, please," Ed ordered his three onlookers. "We need it dark in here. That's one reason why we're not operating from the deck of the *Triton IV*."

Gerlock hastily closed the steel door of the radar shack, to darken the interior. As their eyes became accustomed to the gloom, the television monitoring screens glowed with an eerie green hue. At first the main picture tube seemed empty of any image. Then an ominous black rock, polkadotted with abalone shells, appeared briefly in the beam of the RUM's floodlight.

Ed Morin quickly halted the left track of the RUM while the right track ground forward at half speed. This had the same effect as turning a steering wheel to the left, veering the machine away from the rocky barrier. Not until the floodlights showed a clear path ahead did

Morin restore both tracks to forward gear and full speed ahead.

"You'd think, looking at the screen, that the tractor was on level bottom," Ed Morin said, keeping his full attention glued to his work as he guided the invisible tractor through the deeps in the direction of Sombrero Rock. "Actually, it's heading down a fifty-degree slope."

Tommy said, "The sounding charts show the water goes from zero to six fathoms in the first hundred yards, and it's ten fathoms at the foot of the Rock."

The spectators in the semidark radar hut watched in breathless suspense as the RUM zigzagged its cautious way down the submarine hillside, skidding and slewing at times on the unstable sand bottom. Morin skillfully skirted rock ledges and avoided yawning crevasses the searchlight beam picked up on the monitor screen.

The RUM was brawling its way through a jungle of bladder kelp when Spud and Mr. Kleveland arrived from the beach and joined the others inside the radar hut.

"What would happen," asked the ever-curious Spud as soon as he recovered his breath from his sprint from the beach, "if the coax cable kinked and broke, Ed?"

At the moment Morin's attention was on a black void lying below a rocky cliff-brink on the verge of which he had halted the RUM. A glance at the Geodetic Survey chart of San Miguel Island revealed no deep crevasse at this point, but earthquakes sometimes changed the contours of the ocean bottom in this vicinity overnight.

Extending the electro-mechanical arm to its full fifteen-foot capacity, Ed explored the darkness under the rock rim where the searchlight beam could not reach. Only two feet below, the iron claw kicked up a smudge of sand. Retracting the RUM's exploring mandible, Ed eased the big machine gently off the two-foot "cliff" to a plateau of smooth sand bottom.

"A busted cable," Ed finally answered Spud, "would mean a salvaging job to recover the RUM. But it isn't likely to happen. You notice the RUM isn't dragging its power and control cable behind it; it's laying the coax along its path. It's when I go to bring the RUM back on shore I may have trouble fouling the cable as it rewinds onto the drum. I may even have to have a diver follow the RUM back ashore to make sure the coax doesn't snag on anything. Any volunteers?"

Tommy, suspecting that Ed was giving him an opening to bring up the diving matter, said quickly "I'll do it, Ed. I brought along my scuba and an extra set of bottles.''

In the darkness, Tommy could not see how Gerlock reacted to this news.

A school of strange-looking, silver-sided fish cruised up to the eye of the TV camera, close enough for the viewers to see the delicate undulations of their fins and gills.

Ed Morin was swiveling the camera and lights from side to side now, holding the RUM in second gear, but still heading toward the southeast corner of Sombrero Rock. According to Kurt Gerlock's logbook photocopy, the Spanish galleon *St. Regis* was supposed to be around that corner, on the north side of the Rock.

Everyone was oozing sweat, although it wasn't warm inside the radar shack.

Suddenly Ed Morin switched off all his controls. "It's not the RUM that needs a break, it's me," W6SNI grinned. "I'm bushed, just from concentrating. If I do anything wrong the Union Oil Company would have to replace the RUM—and me as its operator, more than likely.''

The only sign Bonilla and Gerlock gave of the nervous tension they were under was the rapid ticking of the veins in their temples. Gerlock still wore his perpetual grin. Dr. Bonilla kept adjusting his celluloid eye-patch as if the edges cut into his flesh.

When Ed went out for a smoke, Dr. Bonilla appeared to notice the bandage on Tommy's head for the first time.

"Hurt yourself, amigo?'' he inquired solicitously.

Tommy shrugged. "Just where an idea hit me,'' he said. Then, realizing that such feeble Yankee humor might not translate easily to a Spaniard, he went on to explain. "Bumped my head on a stanchion last night. No harm done.''

"To the stanchion?'' Dr. Bonilla quipped, as if to indicate that he, too, had a sense of humor.

Mr. Kleveland was the most nervous one of all. "I wish Ed would keep the ball rolling,'' he grumbled. "Day after tomorrow we've got to be out of here or the Navy will vaporize us with the air-to-ground missiles they're testing out. And Ed stands out there inviting lung cancer.''

As if he had overheard, Ed ground out the stub of his cigarette in the sand and ducked back into the radar hut. Revving up the outside generator again, Morin fed full power back to the RUM and the

TV camera.

While they waited for their eyes to accustom themselves to the dim glow of the television monitor again, Ed said, "You may not think so, but the visibility is phenomenally good down there by Sombrero Rock today—which is a big break in our favor, seeing how limited our time for exploration is. Something you may think is right on top of the RUM may be fifty feet distant."

"I know," Gerlock observed. "Distances are deceptive underwater. I've been diving for thirty years and I still reach for things and find them somewhere else, due to the magnification factor of water."

"Hey, look!" interrupted Spud. "What's that on the screen?"

One half of the TV screen appeared black; the other half was light gray, and showed a pattern of movement like a forest wavering in a windstorm.

"Marine plants on your right, the base of Sombrero Rock on your left, rising out of white sand bottom," Ed interpreted the obscure TV picture, like a surgeon reading an X-ray plate. "I am now going to start the RUM around the corner of the rock. I'd estimate we're still fifty yards away from it."

Sombrero Rock ran off the edge of the monitor and vanished as Ed steered the submarine tractor almost due north. A murmur of excitement passed through the taut-nerved audience as the camera picked up what appeared to be the ribs of a whale—or a sunken ship.

"The phantom galleon!" Spud Kleveland gasped, and consulted his watch to jot down the exact historic moment of the discovery for his newspaper-epic-to-come.

All eyes—including the Cyclopean orb of the RUM—remained focused on the sunken object as the tractor approached it. Tommy glanced at Bonilla and Gerlock. Their faces were slick with perspiration in the eerie witch-glow from the TV tube.

"I'll be willing to bet," thought Tommy, "That no matter what that wreckage turns out to be, Gerlock will identify it as the remains of the *St. Regis*—and pretend to find Cabrillo's lead-plate chart aboard it."

But Tommy was wrong. Gerlock was the first to raise doubts as to the antiquity of the wreckage the tractor had discovered.

"It's too far away from Sombrero Rock to be the galleon," Gerlock pointed out. "Besides, those are the ribs of a much smaller craft than a galleon."

Ed Morin, flashing a quick glance at Tommy that went unnoticed by the others, steered the RUM away from the rotted hulk rather than steamroller it into the sandy floor of the sea.

"That hulk," he said, "belonged to nothing larger than a trawler. Besides, as Mr. Gerlock says, it's too far away from the Rock."

The TV picture was lurching drunkenly now, as the RUM headed across rough bottom. No murder mystery on the late-late show ever gripped its audience in tighter absorption with the plot than did the drama the RUM's closed-circuit TV show revealed to the tense audience in the radar shack.

Ed Morin switched on a second floodlight now. Each could be maneuvered independently of the other. The increased light was a help, for they were sixty feet down now, beyond the reach of daylight.

The light beams moved through a series of Vs and Xs, probing this way and that like the horns of a snail. Details were startlingly clear on the monitor screen now. Thousands of starfish, abalone and other crustaceans scabbed the slimy wall of Sombrero Rock.

The monitor picked up a stingray lying on the bottom, and even a small shark as the tractor pushed on, now paralleling the base of Sombrero Rock only a few yards to the left of the picture.

"It won't be long now," Tommy thought to himself as his excitement grew, "before we've passed the entire north edge of the Sombrero. I wonder what Gerlock will do if the RUM doesn't pick up something he can pretend is the wreck of the—"

The very instant the thought was crossing his mind, Kurt Gerlock almost deafened Tommy with a shout alongside his ear:

"Ed—Ed! Stop the RUM and swing your lights upwards a trifle! Straight ahead, but elevated more—I think I see a large mass of some kind, sort of leaning against the Rock—"

Morin touched knobs and dials in obedience to Gerlock's request, the tiniest of smiles twitching his mouth-corners.

The RUM halted. The funnel-shaped beams of the mercury-vapor searchlights stabbed up into the inky murk at a 50° angle, the two snail's horns of brilliance converging like an X to meet something that obstructed the light as effectively as did the lithic wall of Sombrero Rock on the left, just outside the camera's restricted field of view.

"Focus! Focus!" It was Chester Kleveland shouting now. "Bring whatever it is into sharper focus, can you, Ed?"

Ed Morin touched another button controlling the TV lens.

Tommy Rockford felt his heart almost stop beating as details began to come into sharp resolution on the screen.

Dark rectangles, crisscrossed like windows!

Curlycues that seemed to be—that *were* carved dragons twisted around shields and swords!

A thick, bladelike object resembling a ship's rudder, with kelp growing thickly at its base!

A small black aperture with a tubular object jutting from it, on which Morin now swung the high-intensity quartz halogen lights and shifted the underwater camera's zoom lens for a close-up view.

Tommy couldn't believe his eyes. Of them all, he couldn't credit what he saw on the television screen.

"That's a cannon sticking out of a gun port in a ship's stern!" K6ATX blurted into the vein-pounding hush. "Those carvings—that's the ornamented poop deck of a medieval ship!"

"*The poop of a Spanish galleon*!" Spud put the impossible truth into words. "We've found the *St. Regis.*"

CHAPTER ELEVEN

DIVING TO THE UNKNOWN

Everyone in front of the TV monitor began to shout at once. Spud Kleveland, as deliriously excited as anyone had ever seen him at football games, yelled something in Tommy's ear that sounded like "We were all wrong about everything, weren't we?"

Tommy had no answer for that. There was nothing vague or out of focus about the object that the RUM's camera had located in the mysterious deeps beside Sombrero Rock. There could be no doubt but that the camera was trained on a cannon muzzle projecting from the gun port of a Manila galleon. The ornate wood carvings of the poop, the rudder, even the four-sided stern lantern on the taffrail—these details could not be disputed.

Even Tommy had to confess to himself that while Kurt Gerlock might counterfeit a galleon's logbook, and "discover" a fake chart etched on a sheet of lead, he could hardly produce a Spanish galleon in such an unlikely spot.

When the excitement finally tapered off, Ed Morin's awed voice sounded unnaturally loud in the echo-chamber of the radar hut: "What stumps me is how a galleon could lie submerged for four centuries and still be there. You've got yourself the scoop of the generation, Mr. Kleveland."

Dr. Bonilla, almost incoherent in his excitement, seized Morin's elbow and pointed toward the image on the screen. "Turn your lights above the poop deck, Señor, and beyond—let us see if the mast and rigging are still intact—"

Morin did as he was bid, zooming the lens out to a wide-angle which created the illusion of backing away from the galleon for an overall view of the wreckage rather than a tight close-up of the cannon port.

Taut with suspense, the viewers inside the radar hut kept their eyes glued to the monitor screen as Morin played the RUM's twin searchlights along the starboard side of the sunken hull.

The wreck appeared to be encrusted with the marine deposits of centuries, but the television camera told them one thing for certain: the original disaster, or the effect of time, had destroyed the *St. Regis* from a point just forward of the mizzenmast. The galleon's prow had been reduced to a few barnacle-covered timbers and rotting sections of hull planking.

Only one of the galleon's three masts—the mizzen—was still in evidence, and it had been splintered off at half its original height. Incredibly, the shrouds still formed their tapering cluster of tarred rope ladders leading from the bulwarks to the mizzen top platform where Cabrillo's sailors had once furled canvas.

Chester Kleveland finally groped his way back to reality. Reaching for his wallet, the newspaper publisher dramatically thumbed through it and produced a slip of paper which Tommy recognized as being a certified check from a Santa Bonita bank.

"That picture nets you Payment Number One on our contract, even before you dive down to inspect it, Kurt!" Spud's father said. "At ten thousand dollars, this discovery is a bargain! I'll be the envy of every newspaper in the country—and the best is still to come!"

Tommy expected to see Kurt Gerlock snatch the $10,000 check greedily. Instead, Gerlock pushed it back with the words, "Wait a couple of hours, sir, and make that fifty thousand. See that row of windows on the stern?"

All eyes turned back to the TV picture.

"Clear as a halftone cut!" Kleveland answered.

"Well," Gerlock said smugly, "those windows mark the skipper's cabin of the *St. Regis*! Inside there we'll find the lead plate with the chart marking Cabrillo's grave, I'll gamble on it. But if the stern of the galleon had been destroyed, instead of the prow, I would have been out of luck. As it is, I'll wager that ten thousand dollars you've got in your hand, Mr. Kleveland, that before our time runs out day after tomorrow we'll have Cabrillo's skeleton in armor safely aboard the *Triton IV*."

Dr. Bonilla waggled his head from side to side. "One moment, amigos. Let us not get too excited. That we will probably find Ferrello's lead chart I am fairly confident—but there is a very strong possibility that the tides have long ago washed away that part of the island where Cabrillo's grave was located."

But nothing could quench Kurt Gerlock's optimism now. Turning to Ed Morin, he said, "Let's go put on our diving gear, shall we, and have a look at the galleon? The rest of you keep your eyes on that television screen. The minute we locate that chart, we'll swim out to RUM and wave it in front of the camera, see?"

As Gerlock was heading for the door to get his diving gear, Tommy poked Ed in the ribs to remind him of their agreement of last night.

"Ah—just a moment, sir," Morin called after Gerlock. "I've decided I'll be more useful operating the RUM and the lights than I will as your diving partner. So Tommy Rockford here will substitute for me, if that's okay with you."

For a moment, Gerlock seemed too surprised to react. Then he said dubiously, "I'd prefer to go alone than have an inexperienced boy to be responsible for, Ed. No offense to you, Tommy, but those are pretty dangerous waters out there, and—"

Morin, taking his cue from Tommy, said adamantly, "I'm sorry, sir, but I can't permit you to swim out to the galleon alone. It's against all safety practice in diving. Any number of things could endanger your life. A rotten plank might cave under your weight and trap you beyond the limit of air in your scuba bottles. To say nothing of manta rays and killer sharks and moray eels and the routine hazards of diving in these waters."

There was a moment's silence, and then Mr. Kleveland said "I'm responsible for Tommy's safety too, Ed. Are you sure he's qualified to accompany Gerlock?"

The look Ed flashed in Tommy's direction said as plainly as words, "We've found the galleon, so doesn't that nullify your suspicions that this deal isn't on the level?" But Tommy's set jaw and scowling brows told him that the boy was still determined that somebody be present when Gerlock located the Cabrillo chart, so he said "As Tommy's diving instructor, Mr. Kleveland, I assure you he's fully competent. After all, he's been much farther down than ten fathoms, which is the depth of the *St. Regis*."

Gerlock said, "Okay, okay, we're wasting time, see? Let's go."

Tommy's scuba equipment was on the *Galloping Goose;* Gerlock had unloaded his on the beach earlier in the day. As Tommy headed for the launch, Spud raced out to catch up with him.

"You're convinced now you're mistaken about things, aren't you?" Spud inquired anxiously. "I mean, the galleon is there; you saw it with your own eyes!"

Sitting down on a driftlog to take off his shoes and socks preparatory to wading out to the *Galloping Goose,* Tommy put into words a conviction that had been growing on him of recent minutes. "I've changed my mind about Gerlock, yes—but I still think Bonilla is a phoney. As for going with Gerlock to the galleon—it's not because I think the lead plate chart is a phoney, Spud. It's because I wouldn't miss diving to a Spanish galleon for a million dollars!"

Aboard the launch, Tommy upended his duffle bag and carefully checked each item of his diving gear—swimming fins, snorkle, face mask, waterproof flashlight, emergency knife, weight belt, and the mouthpiece, breathing hoses, pressure gauge, air valve and dual air bottles of his scuba.

Stripping to the skin, Tommy climbed into the foam rubber diving suit he had rented from Don Duckett's Diver's Den the day before. Called a "wet suit" because water was allowed to enter it, the foam rubber garment was preferred over the pure rubber "dry suit" by most of Southern California's scuba enthusiasts.

For one thing, it did away with wearing itchy woolen underwear to keep warm; the small amount of seawater allowed inside a wet suit quickly warmed to body temperature and served as an insulator in addition to the foam neoprene itself.

Since foam rubber had only a third of the stretch of pure rubber, it was more easily torn; but a ripped suit would not mean loss of buoyancy, since that was built into the suit itself in the form of millions of tiny nitrogen bubbles impregnated into the neoprene rubber.

After donning the suit, Tommy snapped on his swim fins and fitted the glass-fronted face mask over his nose and eyes.

The scuba—short for Self-Contained Underwater Breathing Apparatus—came next. It consisted of twin bottles of air, compressed to 2,250 pounds per square inch, filtered to make sure of its purity, with intake and exhaust hoses and a rubber mouthpiece through which the diver inhaled and exhaled.

As the last step, Tommy buckled on his weights, a belt which carried heavy lead wafers to counteract his tendancy to float and give him neutral buoyancy when he got underwater. Tommy had telephoned his current weight to Don Duckett at the Diver's Den yesterday afternoon, so the belt could be "tailored" to fit him.

When Tommy waded ashore he found Gerlock fitted out in his Italian-model rubber dry suit. Tommy noted with a stab of nervous apprehension that Gerlock was carrying a diver's spear gun—a deadly spring-powered weapon with a pistol grip at one end and a needle-sharp, three-pronged trident or harpoon attached to the barrel.

One touch of the hair trigger could release that spear with force enough to impale a large shark...or a husky teenager.

Looking at the lethal gun in Gerlock's hand, Tommy was reminded of his conviction that someone—perhaps Gerlock—had knocked him overboard to drown out in the Channel last night.

If Gerlock would attempt murder aboard the *Triton IV,* what would stop him from firing that spear gun at Tommy, once they got under the ocean where no witnesses could see the act committed? No one could ever prove that such a tragedy wasn't accidental...

"I'm letting my imagination run away with me," Tommy said to himself, and with a supreme effort of will power, he forced himself to banish such negative thoughts from his mind. Any diver entering waters where he might meet up with a shark or a barracuda would be foolish not to carry a weapon of some sort.

As the two divers came abreast of the radar hut where the others were waiting, Ed Morin came out to check their breathing apparatus and make sure the gauges registered a full charge of compressed air.

Ed's face was gaunt from nervous strain and his eyes were frankly worried as he came over to inspect Tommy's scuba. In a voice pitched for Tommy alone, Morin said, "Use the RUM coax cable as a guide out to the galleon, Tommy. Don't try to beeline for Sombrero Rock, even if Gerlock does. The currents are tricky out there. You could get lost and swept out to sea very easily. I—I wish you'd change your mind about going, Tommy."

Tommy said, "I'm no longer suspicious about Gerlock trying to sneak a counterfeit lead plate out there, Ed—but I wouldn't miss this opportunity for the world."

Spud Kleveland came out to stand beside the two divers as his father took several flash shots of them, presumably being interviewed by the *News-Star* reporter.

"Your ears!" Spud cried. "You aren't wearing ear plugs, Tommy! Neither are you, Mr. Gerlock!"

Ed Morin commented drily, "I see you have a lot to learn about skin-diving, son. If you wear plugs, an air pocket is formed between your eardrum and the plug. When you descend, you equalize the pressure in your eustachian tubes and inner ear to the same pressure as the outside water."

"I know all that—think I'm stupid?" complained Spud, who had a rather exalted opinion of his own knowledge.

"What you obviously don't know," Morin retorted, "is that the air pocket on the outside of the eardrums remains at a constant pressure due to the plug's stopping the outside water pressure. That puts too much force on the inside of the eardrum, and can rupture it. Even at a depth of ten feet. And Tommy and Mr. Gerlock will be diving to sixty feet. The pressure down there is three times what it is on the surface."

Spud's cheeks went scarlet. "I'm sorry," he mumbled. "Mr. Know-it-all might get himself drowned sometime for being smart."

Everyone came over to shake hands with the two divers, as if they were astronauts about to climb into the space shuttle before taking off for outer space.

Then, accompanied only by Mr. Kleveland and his video tape recorder, Tommy and Gerlock flapped off along the beach to the point where the RUM's coaxial cable entered the surf.

When they reached the edge of the water, Gerlock turned to Tommy and, shouting to make himself heard above the wind and surf, said, "We're going down sixty feet, see? You understand our safe submersion time can be no more than fifty-five minutes without decompression stops on the way out?"

Tommy nodded. "My watch is waterproof. I'll keep track of the time."

Gerlock went on, "You understand when we ascend, we do not exceed a rate of twenty-five feet per minute? To come up any faster would be inviting a bad case of the bends, see?"

Again Tommy nodded.

"Then follow me. Stay behind me at all times, see? This spear gun is no toy. I don't want any accidents."

"I sure agree with you there, sir."

"Okay. Let's go. We're about to make history, see?"

Tommy, with barely a year's diving experience with scuba—seventeen was the minimum age a skin diver could graduate to scuba in Southern California—was glad to have a professional of Gerlock's long experience to show him the proper place to enter the surf. He had been skin diving with a snorkel for years, and he knew that entry was always a dangerous moment in any diving activity.

The surf was heavy and breaking close to shore, indicating a steep beach, as the RUM had already ascertained and as the mariners' charts indicated. Rip currents, which caused eight out of ten accidents to the skin-diving community, were to be dreaded most, far more than kelp entanglements.

At waist depth the two inserted their mouthpieces between their teeth and each turned on the other's air valves. Then, with a final adjustment of shoulder harness and a check of their knives and flashlights, the two exchanged nods to indicate that each was in readiness to submerge.

Behind them on the beach, Chester Kleveland's portable video recorder followed the two as they turned to face a huge green breaker rolling in from the northeast. The wave engulfed them in a mountainous avalanche of brine, with a roar like a thousand express trains.

A vicious undertow seized their legs—a terrifying thing for the ordinary surf swimmer, for it sucked them along the sloping bottom and dumped them over the brink of a submarine cliff without a chance. Carrying their own air supply, however, they had no cause for alarm.

For every foot of depth, the pressure increased by a little less than a half pound per square inch. Tommy took comfort in the reassuring hiss of air from the bottles strapped to his back, the bubbles leaving the scuba exhaust hose making a musical gurgling in his ears.

Tommy and Kurt Gerlock were lost in the dark, mysterious and silent world of the ocean depths now, a sensation which no landsman could understand without sharing the experience.

With breast stroke and flippers the two divers angled like air gliders suspended in space, trailing chains of silver bubbles as they propelled themselves onward and downward.

Fish darted about them, curious about these two-legged interlopers from another world. Tommy kept close behind Gerlock, timing the rhythm of his own swimming stroke to his partner's. It soon became evident that Tommy would need years of practice before he could knife through the blue-green void of King Neptune's realm with the speed and effortless ease Gerlock was demonstrating.

Tommy lost track of time or depth. He had forgotten Ed's admonition to follow the RUM's cable out to the wreck; he was depending on Kurt Gerlock's orientation alone.

Increasing coldness and pressure told him they had reached and passed the thirty-three foot mark, where atmospheric pressure was exactly doubled to about thirty pounds per square inch.

He followed Gerlock through a jungle of bladder kelp—panicky stuff to get tangled up in, with or without scuba.

And then, a ghostly glow off in the watery distance, Tommy saw the pale white nimbus of light that marked the twin searchlights on the RUM tractor, playing their dazzling fingers over and around the phantom galleon.

CHAPTER TWELVE

A PUZZLING DISCOVERY

Twenty-one of their allotted fifty-five minutes of submersion time had elapsed before Gerlock and Tommy swam into the field of vision of the RUM's television eye.

Both swimmers were tired from their silent battle with cross-currents and rocky bottom, so the quiet waters in the lee of Sombrero Rock came as a welcome relief.

Ed Morin blinked a small signal lamp on the port side of the tractor to spell out in Morse code EVERYTHING A-OK?

Tommy glanced at Gerlock, who shrugged to indicate he did not understand. Removing his flashlight from its belt clip, Tommy aimed it at the TV camera and flashed back, ALL A-OK. PSE BLINK FLOODLITES IN TWENTY MINUTES TO WARN US ABOUT AIR SUPPLY.

By the time Morin had blinked back the letter R to indicate "message received," Gerlock had started up toward the looming poop deck of the galleon, gliding weightlessly through the murky depths as if using the tilted searchlight beam for a grand staircase.

The *St. Regis* had been a triple-deck galleon, and its huge size astonished Tommy. The TV camera's wide-angle lens had reduced the apparent dimensions of the wreck as seen on the screen. Now that he stood beside it, Tommy realized that the vertical distance from the sandy ocean bottom to the ornamental lantern on the stern was the height of a three-story building, or halfway to the surface.

Tommy noted that Gerlock was holding his rate of climb to the safe twenty-five feet per minute, actually timing himself with his waterproof wristwatch. The decompression represented by even that short distance amounted to a hazard which, if he rose too quickly, could put nitrogen bubbles into the bloodstream like the carbonation in soda pop, resulting in the agonizing and often fatal "bends."

As Tommy followed Gerlock in a slow ascent of the face of the galleon's ornately decorated stern, Ed Morin in the radar hut on shore was maneuvering the RUM tractor to the west, so as to bathe the wreck in the white, eerie glow of the mercury-vapor lamps from a side angle.

This side-lighting threw the wood carvings into bold relief, enabling Tommy and Gerlock to recognize the design even under the incrustations of slime and fungus.

They made out dragons wrapped around broadswords, and at the top, just under the ornamental lantern, a shield bearing a coat of arms which Tommy guessed was either the heraldic emblem of the owner of the ship or the insignia of *St. Regis,* the patron saint for whom the galleon had been named.

Reaching out to examine a projecting bit of carving—the head of one of the dragons—Tommy was dismayed to have it crumble like wet sugar in his grasp, so completely had it been undermined by the borings of toredo worms.

A sharp tapping noise reached his eardrums, and Tommy turned to see that Kurt Gerlock was signaling by rapping his spear gun against his scuba bottle. The diver shook his head vigorously and pointed to the wooden decorations, by way of warning Tommy not to handle them.

They knew that Chester Kleveland had high hopes of raising the hulk as an historic curiosity, but if the whole ship was as decayed as the wood carvings, salvage would be impossible; the hull would be sliced in two by the lift of the hoisting cables.

Moments later, kicking their rubber flippers to propel them up and over the ornate railing at the top level, the two divers found themselves floating horizontally, parallel to the top deck and outside the direct glare of floodlights from the RUM.

This meant they were no longer visible to the televiewers in the radar hut ashore. If Gerlock had brought along that spear gun with murder in mind, this was an ideal opportunity to use it. But now that the discovery of the galleon had removed his suspicions concerning Gerlock's honesty, Tommy felt no anxiety at all.

Gerlock had his flashlight on now, playing its puny cone of light over the deck below. It was slimy with the siltation and marine deposits of the years, but when their flippers came to rest on the planking, the wreck felt as solid as the wall of Sombrero Rock against which the *St. Regis* rested. The galleon had settled on her keel and remained so nearly upright that they were only faintly aware of a list to the port side.

A flight of wooden steps led from the elevated poop deck to the main deck amidships. Tommy, not used to the underwater life, headed toward the stairs as if they were the only way to go below. Gerlock, as a matter of habit, took the beeline distance, as a fish might.

They allowed their own weight to drift them silently to the deck below. At first it puzzled Tommy to see squares of illumination from the RUM's floodlights pouring fanwise onto the amidships portion of the wreck. Then he realized that the light was coming through the stern windows of the captain's cabin, and that there was no forward bulkhead or fourth wall to shut off the light.

At this close range, the divers could see where a fire had gutted the *St. Regis,* for the stubs of ribs curving up from the sand-covered keel were black with charcoal, as were the ends of the deck plankings.

Why, Tommy wondered subconsciously, hadn't a fire at sea been mentioned in the logbook's account of the end of the galleon?

At the moment he gave the subject no further thought, for Gerlock was beckoning him forward. They were about to enter the captain's quarters—an easy task, since the partitioning bulkhead was missing.

What, Tommy wondered, would they do if the lead plate chart had been bolted to the missing bulkhead? It could have been destroyed by the fire which had obviously consumed the forward part of the ship before it sank.

No matter how many times he dived, Tommy Rockford could never get over the weird exhilaration of finding himself weightless, able to propel himself with the slightest movement of his flippers or hands. He imagined it was similar to the sensations experienced by astronauts in outer space.

Swimming with gentle strokes, avoiding any contact with the timbering of the galleon lest they bring the upper deck crashing down to trap them in the wreckage, Gerlock and Tommy floated into the Spanish captain's cabin side by side.

The RUM's television floodlights converted the four square

windows into white rectangles, too blinding to look at directly. The floodlight beams, entering from a lower angle, distinctly illuminated the beamed ceiling and a corroded brass lantern which hung at a slight angle from a bracket.

The ghostly reflected light filled the galleon's cabin, and brought to Tommy, at least, a distinct sense of disappointment and let-down.

He had imagined that the *St. Regis,* sinking so rapidly, would be crammed with furniture, if not treasure—he seemed to recall that the ship had been empty of cargo on its voyage to the island to recover Cabrillo's remains in 1581. But the interior of the cabin seemed stripped of all furnishings except the small cannon, the muzzle of which they had seen from the outside.

There were no exotic sea chests, or sextants, or racks of rusting cutlasses, or muskets, or any other trappings which Tommy Rockford had pictured inside a Spanish galleon of 1581.

"Someone," he thought despairingly, "has been here ahead of us. Unless the currents which washed out the bulkhead also stripped out the moveable objects..."

Gerlock, eerily suspended between deck and ceiling, was starting to make a circuit of the port, starboard and stern walls of the cabin, using his flashlight to study every square foot of wall space.

Gerlock was, of course, searching for the chunk of lead which was supposed to be bolted to the bulkhead, according to the old Minorcan's logbook entry.

While Gerlock was busy on that detail, Tommy swam over to the cannon, a small one mounted on a carriage with wooden disks for wheels, its nose jutting out the small, square port in the stern.

Removing his knife from its scabbard, Tommy squatted down to scratch at the breech end of the cannon, intending to remove the outer coating of sludge and corrosion to determine whether it was made of brass or of iron.

To his astonishment, the knife blade sank easily into the cannon— to the depth of an inch or more.

Assuming that the soft material was a marine deposit of some kind—it could be animal, vegetable or mineral—Tommy had another try with the knife.

This time, a v-shaped chip was freed of the cannon barrel and went floating away.

"Now this is what Spud would call a ding-dong doozie-roo of

a puzzle," raced the thought through Tommy's brain. "This cannon is made of wood instead of metal!"

So absorbed was Tommy in his inspection of the dummy cannon that he was unaware of Gerlock swimming over behind him. It was the touch of Gerlock's elbow on his shoulder that startled Tommy into almost losing his grip on the mouthpiece of his breathing hose. His first thought was that an inquisitive shark had nosed him from behind.

Instead he saw that it was Kurt Gerlock, making excited gestures for him to follow.

Swimming after Gerlock, Tommy saw his diving partner focus the white spot of his flashlight beam on a dark rectangle on the stern bulkhead, above the level of the windows. When Gerlock tapped the dark rectangle with the blunt handle of his speargun, the faint thud of hard metal on soft metal was transmitted to Tommy's ears.

Tommy swam in close, peering at the object through his face plate. It was about eight by ten inches in size, and about a quarter of an inch thick. Black in color, it was fixed to the wooden bulkhead with heavy green-corroded bronze screws.

Cabrillo's grave chart!

Only the fact that both of them had to keep their teeth clamped on the mouthpieces of their scuba kept them from shouting the words to each other.

This was what they had dived into the unknown to find.

This was the map that would unlock the secret of the centuries on San Miguel Island.

Sheathing his knife, Tommy used his free hand to reach up and rub the metal plate. His sensitive fingertips made out deep indentations in the metal surface.

Gerlock held his flashlight beam parallel to the plane of the lead plate, to put the carved incisions into relief. There was no mistaking the deeply cut triangular outlines of San Miguel, with the familiar indentation that was Cuyler Harbor.

Along the lower edge of the lead plate was an inscription, perfectly legible when the flashlight beam hit it at an angle:

ISLA DE POSESION A.D. 1543. BF FECIT

Isla de Posesion—that was the name Juan Rodriguez Cabrillo had given to the island where his two caravals had anchored in the fall of 1542.

"BF FECIT"—Latin for "B.F. made it." B.F. could only be Cabrillo's chief pilot and successor as captain of the expedition, Bartolome Ferrello.

Only the cold water kept Tommy's cheeks from burning with shame. This lead plate was firmly fastened to the wood; Gerlock hadn't smuggled it down here hidden in his diving suit, so as to have a counterfeit with which to bilk Mr. Kleveland out of $40,000.

Both divers, having found what they came for, were now reminded that their worst enemy, time, was running against them. A glance at their watches confirmed this—they had been down thirty-three minutes. That left them with barely enough time to get back to shore, assuming that the currents would benefit instead of impede them, as it had on the swim out.

Gerlock handed Tommy his flashlight, signaling for him to direct both beams on the lead plate.

Then, using the speargun's tip as a lever, Gerlock attempted to pry the lead plate off the wall. Both knew there was not enough time to attempt to loosen the screws, which would probably disintegrate when touched with a tool anyway.

The soft lead was easily damaged. After a couple of minutes' work, Gerlock succeeded in getting the upper right corner free of the screw. With one corner loosened, it was easy now to work the sharp point of the speargun's trident behind the lead plate and peel it backward away from the bulkhead planks.

When the lead plate finally came free, Gerlock hugged it against his chest, and then motioned for Tommy to return the flashlight.

That done, Gerlock made the "let's surface" gesture by jerking his thumb upward.

Tommy nodded to indicate that he had received the order and would obey it.

With the sudden darting motion of a fish, Gerlock swam out through one of the four-foot-square windows, into the dazzling beam of the RUM's floodlights.

Tommy saw Gerlock's grotesque shadow projected against the water as he fulfilled his promise to their friends on shore, swimming down toward the TV camera and holding out the lead plate to let them know their mission was successfully completed.

Only the fact that he knew his air supply was running out kept

Tommy from doing some more exploring inside the captain's cabin. The bronze ceiling lantern would make a wonderful souvenir, and so would the wooden-barreled cannon.

But the air was coming through the hoses with more difficulty now, warning Tommy that he would soon have to reach for the valve and "crack the by-pass" to admit his reserve supply of air.

Swimming out through the same window by which Gerlock had made his exit, Tommy found the blinding lights too much for his eyes. To avoid the white glare, he swam straight for the bottom, out of their direct beams.

When his flippers touched bottom he had a look at his watch, as soon as his eyes returned to normal.

Nine minutes left—and it had taken them twenty-one minutes to swim out here, bucking the currents. Well, he had waited too long, but he could always head straight for the surface and swim the rest of the way ashore. That way, he was only sixty feet away from fresh air—although to surface would mean having to fight the heavy waves, which were not noticeable on the bottom.

Directly in front of Tommy was the huge rudder post of the galleon, almost invisible behind the shadows of the bladder kelp which grew between it and the RUM tractor.

In the act of turning away to avoid the kelp, Tommy saw something between the rudder and the hull which roused his curiosity. Before he surfaced, he had to find out whether that object was what it appeared to be, or whether the distortion of vision at this depth had tricked his eyes.

At that very moment, Ed Morin winked the RUM's lights on and off three times—the warning signal that their air supply was nearing the danger point.

Tommy peered around, wondering where Gerlock was, but saw no sign of his diving partner.

Swimming back around the kelp and into the field of view of the TV camera, Tommy pointed his flashlight at the RUM and flashed a blinker signal in Morse: WHERE'S GERLOCK?

Ed Morin flashed in reply: HEADED FOR SHORE. TAKE OFF TOMMY. AIR SUPPLY ABOUT GONE.

Tommy waved to indicate he understood. But instead of swimming away from the galleon's rudder, he headed toward it, out of sight of the televiewers and behind the curtain of kelp.

Tommy's flashlight probed into the shadows behind the rudder. The thing he thought he had seen was a propeller—which was of course preposterous. Manila galleons sailed the Pacific in the 1500's; the screw propeller hadn't even been invented for another three hundred years.

Swimming in for a close look, Tommy felt the blood turn cold in his veins.

His first glimpse had been correct. There was a propeller behind this galleon's rudder—a three-bladed, thirty-inch screw, green with corrosion, connected to a propeller shaft which vanished into a modern gasketed bushing bolted to the pulp-rotten planking of the *St. Regis's* hull.

Tommy Rockford couldn't explain it, and he doubted if his friends on shore would believe it, but the truth was inescapable.

The phantom galleon was a hoax.

CHAPTER THIRTEEN

SECRET OF THE CENTURIES

The implications of his discovery stunned K6ATX. To find a modern-day propeller on a galleon which was supposed to have collided with Sombrero Rock more than four centuries in the past was more than the boy's imagination could cope with.

It was the on-and-off blinking of the RUM's powerful searchlights which brought Tommy back to reality. Ed Morin must be getting worried now, for he had watched Tommy swim over to the rudder of the *St. Regis,* behind masking kelp, and had not seen what became of him. More than one diver had been trapped and drowned in kelp.

Tommy swam back into the glare of lights, to see the RUM tractor lurching toward him, metal treads stirring up a smudge of disturbed sand and seashells. The iron monster halted when its television eye picked up the object of its search, and then the signal lamp winked, YOU HAVEN'T TIME TO SWIM ASHORE. YOUR AIR SUPPLY DANGEROUSLY LOW. ADVISE YOU SWIM AROUND SOMBRERO ROCK AND THEN SURFACE. WILL PICK YOU UP OUTSIDE BAR WITH LAUNCH. OK?

Tommy knew the zoom lens of the TV camera was focused on him now, meaning that his head and shoulders filled the monitor screen on shore. He nodded vigorously, then pointed to the by-pass valve of his scuba to indicate that he still had his two-minute air reserve left.

Morin's blinker came back: GET GOING. 73.

Tommy turned and began swimming toward the near corner of Sombrero Rock, Morin obligingly swinging the RUM around so as to give him the benefit of the mercury-vapor searchlights.

He was breathing with increasing difficulty by the time he had rounded the shoulder of Sombrero Rock, a positive sign that the pressure in his air bottles was dangerously low. He reached up to crack the by-pass valve and inhaled with relief as the reserve air came hissing through the hoses.

Two short minutes and his reserve would be exhausted—and from six fathoms down he needed that much time just to reach the surface without risking the bends.

Tommy unbuckled his weight belt to give him extra buoyancy and started his ascent. On the inshore side of Sombrero Rock the water was turbulent, but every foot of altitude gained meant a corresponding lessening of pressure, which was in his favor.

"Never get ahead of your bubbles" was the rule divers used to control their rate of ascent. This was the first time Tommy had ever been in an emergency situation this far under, and he had to keep a tight rein on his self-control to avoid panicking.

The water was getting lighter in color, and appreciably warmer. He could feel the pressure lessening on his ears. Once above the critical thirty-three-foot mark, which was the region of exactly doubled pressure, Tommy knew he could make it.

The sunlighted surface of the ocean was visible through his face plate now. His lungs felt close to bursting by the time his head broke surface and he could spit out the mouthpiece and suck in a lifesaving lungful of air.

Treading water, Tommy had a look around. Behind him was the sheer wall of Sombrero Rock. Not twenty yards inshore the surf was thundering on the harbor bar.

A flash of sunlight on windshield glass directed his eyes to the welcome sight of the good old *Galloping Goose* planing through the white turbulence that marked the Devil's Jaw. The launch swung toward him as Ed Morin spotted Tommy's head and gunned his inboard engine to full throttle, his speed leaving a high rooster-tail of spray in his wake.

Up here on the surface, waiting for his pick-up boat, an eerie feeling of unreality came over Tommy Rockford. He had the strange sensation that he had just awakened from a bad dream, and that the experiences he had undergone on the bottom were no more real than the hallucinations of nitrogen narcosis which deep-sea divers know as "rapture of the deep."

Moments later the *Galloping Goose* was alongside and Ed was hauling him aboard, obviously relieved that his friend's dive was over.

"Gerlock's just coming out of the surf," Morin commented, gesturing toward shore. "That fellow must scoot through the water like a porpoise. He didn't have any more air supply than you did, and he had a lot farther to go."

Ed helped Tommy remove his scuba harness. On shore, Tommy could see Mr. Kleveland's flash gun blinking as he took pictures of Gerlock emerging from the ocean, draped with kelp and hugging the precious lead plate to his chest.

Spud was recording the big event with his father's video-tape camera while Dr. Bonilla waded out into knee-deep water to greet his partner.

"You came up too fast, kid," Ed Morin said. "You look bad."

Tommy shook his head. "I feel fine," he said, "but I—I had a funny thing happen down there, Ed. I'd like to tell you about it—before we go back into the harbor."

Ed was concerned by the haunted look he saw mirrored in Tommy's eyes. Sometimes divers suffer brain damage if they remain submerged too long.

"Let's get into the cabin out of this wind," Ed suggested, "and you can talk it out while you peel off that rubber suit. The duds you were wearing yesterday are dried out by now."

After waving to the others on the beach to let them know he was safely aboard Ed's launch, Tommy ducked into the cabin just as Ed was swinging the helm hard aport to keep the *Goose* going in circles.

"Is what you're going to tell me connected with your reason for insisting on diving with Gerlock today?" Ed asked.

"Very much so," Tommy said, as Ed helped him remove the clammy neoprene suit. "You see, I thought Gerlock was going to smuggle a counterfeit lead plate down there and pretend he found it on the galleon. Well, I was wrong on that score. I stood by while he pried it off the bulkhead with his speargun. But I discovered something about that galleon that has me scared stiff, Ed."

"I'm all ears, kid. You don't *look* scared. Just nervous."

Ed Morin kept his attention on the whitecaps outside, to make sure the *Galloping Goose* kept clear of the rocks, but gave Tommy a nod to start talking.

"I might as well begin at the beginning and tell you why I flew to California in the first place," K6ATX said, and he began by telling of Spud's telegram inviting him to go on the San Miguel expedition, and his curiosity over Dr. Bonilla's being in Santa Bonita with the Klevelands when Tommy himself had worked him on ham radio in Seville, Spain.

Now, for the first time, Tommy gave voice to his secret hunch that his falling overboard from the *Triton IV* the night before had been a deliberate attack, not an accident.

Ed Morin listened in fascinated silence during the time it took Tommy to wriggle back into his underwear, T-shirt and blue jeans. Then he said gravely, "It would seem as if Gerlock and this Bonilla, or Lou Weber, are trying to swindle some money out of Chet Kleveland. Confidence men always insist on strict secrecy, they tell me. But one thing knocks the props out from under your whole story, Tommy."

"Finding the Spanish galleon?"

"Exactly. They couldn't have faked that."

Then Tommy dropped his big bombshell:

"I don't know how they did it, but they did. Ed, that galleon has a bronze propeller behind the rudder! Three-bladed. A good thirty inches in diameter."

Ed's jaw sagged open in disbelief. "The heck you say! Propellers weren't even invented until 1804 or thereabouts—and the galleon sank in 1581!"

Tommy grinned bleakly. "Sort of jolts you, doesn't it? I won't believe it's really there till I go down for another look—this time with a Leica camera, to prove it to Ross Jackson."

Ed stood there leaning against the radio compass, shaking his head from side to side in stunned disbelief.

"We'd better get ashore, I guess," Tommy said, noticing that the shore party had assembled at the radar hut. "Don't breathe a word of what I've told you to Mr. Kleveland, now. I want to radio Ross Jackson first and let him handle it."

Ed spun the wheel and reached for the throttle, to send the *Galloping Goose* toward the narrow, rock-ribbed entrance of the Devil's Jaw. Even in a shallow draft launch, it was a touch-and-go operation threading the needle's eye into the harbor.

"Kleveland wants me to leave the RUM down below over tomorrow," Ed said, "because he wants Gerlock to take photographs of the galleon from all angles and will need my TV lights. Tomorrow I aim to have a look at that propeller of yours, Tommy, just to make sure it isn't depth-sickness on your part."

Tommy grinned. "You'll see it, all right. And another thing. You know that cannon muzzle the TV camera picked up? Well, that cannon is made of wood. I cut a chip out of it with my diver's knife and saw it float away."

The two swayed drunkenly as the launch was caught in the foaming surf of the Devil's Jaw. When they were safe inside the harbor again, Ed answered, "A dummy cannon doesn't jar me too much, Tommy. I understand ships used to use fake cannons in the old days, to make pirates think they carried more firepower than they actually did. Or maybe it was just intended for ornamental purposes, like the carved dragons and things."

Further discussion was precluded by their arrival at the beach, where their four companions were already wading out to the launch.

Chester Kleveland's expression showed Tommy that the Santa Bonita publisher was in seventh heaven over the sensational find Gerlock had made aboard the *St. Regis*. Tommy knew it was a chunk of lead worth perhaps two dollars at a junk yard—but worth $40,000 to Kurt Gerlock unless Tommy could circumvent the conspiracy.

Tommy helped Spud and the portable video recorder aboard. Gerlock, who had left his scuba bottles and spear gun in the radar shack, was still encased in his shiny black suit. He had relinquished the lead plate to Dr. Bonilla, who was carrying it as gingerly as if it had been a butterfly's wing.

Chester Kleveland, his arms loaded with camera equipment, was hovering alongside Dr. Bonilla like a bodyguard protecting the Crown Jewels of England.

"I don't see how I'm going to get a picture of the map that I can reproduce in a newspaper," he was saying as the two clambered aboard. "The lines on the chart are just black on dark gray—"

"Ah," Bonilla answered, "I will show you how that is done in my museum, señor. We take photographs every day of old documents much worse than this lead plate."

All was happy confusion during the few minutes it took Ed to maneuver the *Galloping Goose* alongside the barge. From what Tommy could gather, the Cabrillo chart Gerlock had removed from the galleon bulkhead was crammed with detail despite its immersion in salt water, presumably for over four hundred years.

Alone of the group, Ed Morin and Tommy Rockford had reason to believe that Gerlock had secreted the lead plate on the sunken wreck perhaps within the past few weeks. For if the galleon was a counterfeit, the lead plate would also be spurious.

All had ravenous appetites. In the excitement of the day's activities, no one had had time to realize that they had not eaten since breakfast, an eternity ago.

Captain Tucker had a happy surprise awaiting them—a hot meal which he had prepared after catching up on his lost sleep.

Hungry as they were, everyone was eager to get the sludge cleaned off the lead plate so as to examine the chart and its instructions on how to locate Cabrillo's long-lost grave. This, even the impatient Chester Kleveland agreed, was a very critical and delicate task, best left to the expert professional talents of Dr. Bonilla.

In lieu of a laboratory, Dr. Bonilla elected to use the *Triton IV's* galley pantry. The sheet of lead was tenderly placed in a large flat pan, while a kettle of water was set on an electric hot plate to come to a boil.

"Ordinary soap and warm water is what we will use to clean this priceless object," Dr. Bonilla told his audience, sluicing fresh tap water into the tray to cover the dirt-encrusted lead plate. "We cannot use a wire brush, of course, because the lead is so soft, and even a toothbrush might damage it. But it is fortunate for us that Bartolome Ferrello used lead, for had he drawn his chart on copper, the sea water would have long since eroded it."

Water from the kettle on the electric plate brought the cleaning solution to the temperature Dr. Bonilla required. If he was actually a confidence man named Lou Weber, he was a very skilled actor; his every movement was that of a scientist engaged on a very painstaking job.

Dr. Bonilla used successive changes of warm, soapy water to clean the lead plate. Soon the triangular outline of San Miguel Island was distinctly visible. Covering the north central part of the island was a series of zigzag marks, each with compass bearings indicated.

"You see," Dr. Bonilla went on to explain, "all the Manila galleons carried large quantities of sheet lead on their voyages—not for trading purposes, but for—"

"For ballast," cut in Spud, always quick to display his learning.

"Wrong, my boy," Dr. Bonilla put Spud in his place. "Galleons used rocks and sand for ballast. The sheet lead was for making emergency hull patches at sea, far from a drydock. If a galleon punched a hole in her hull under the waterline, a diver would go down with a sheet of this lead and the terrific suction of inflowing water would plaster the lead tightly against the hull and seal the leak until permanent repairs could be made."

Having sponged off the lead plate to his satisfaction, Dr. Bonilla dried it with paper towels and set it aside on the galley table. Rummaging in the galley cabinets, he brought forth a box of cornstarch, which he proceeded to dust over the lead plate until it was completely covered.

"And now," Dr. Bonilla told the puzzled audience, "we will show you how to prepare this map for a photograph, señores."

So saying, he proceeded to brush off the excess cornstarch with a towel, leaving the scratches on the lead plate standing out in vivid white against the dull black of the metal.

"Why, that'll photograph perfectly!" exulted Chester Kleveland. "Don't anybody shake the starch out of those lines and letters until I've had a chance to take some close-up shots. Archaeologists all over the country will want prints of this."

Spud, showing his innate talent for journalism, announced proudly, "My story is going to bill it as the most exciting discovery since the Rosetta Stone."

While Mr. Kleveland was out getting his camera equipment, the others crowded around the table to study the map. The zigzag line which represented the path Cabrillo's Spaniards had taken in 1542 to reach the explorer's grave—probably a sheer invention of either Bonilla or Gerlock—started at a point midway along the crescent curve of Cuyler Harbor's beach and ended at a deeply-incised Maltese cross, representing the grave site, at what appeared to be the summit of the island.

Each zig and zag was indicated with compass bearings.

"We have two more full days left before our permit from the Navy expires," Gerlock announced, "and I would say it's going to take two days to retrace the route on this map. At each change of direction on the map we'll have to take new compass readings—and hope the distances indicated on the map haven't been altered by erosion and landslides and such."

Tommy stepped out on deck to join Ed Morin.

"What do you make of it?" Ed asked. "Gerlock's talking as if the map actually will lead us to Cabrillo's grave."

"It would be easier to lead us to a human skeleton," Tommy said, "than to a Spanish galleon. And those bones would be worth another fifty thousand dollars to Gerlock, so you can rest assured we'll at least dig up a skull."

They went back inside to see Mr. Kleveland take close-up photographs of the chart, which remained in the cook's pan, placed on the floor of the galley pantry with the press camera, mounted on a tripod, positioned directly above it.

When Kleveland had all the still shots he wanted, he opened his wallet with a flourish and, turning to Gerlock, handed him two certified checks.

"Ten thousand for locating the galleon—forty thousand for locating Ferrello's chart," the publisher of the *News-Star* said grandiloquently. "Cheap enough, I would say, for the biggest archaeological find of the century."

Tommy muttered to Ed, "Change that 'find' to 'hoax' and he'd be closer to the truth."

Ed answered, "The plotters have been paid off. Want to bet they'll make some excuse to visit Santa Bonita tomorrow—before Mr. Kleveland's had time to track down Cabrillo's grave?"

Tommy smiled grimly. "I'm radioing the sheriff tonight," he said, "to fly out here and arrest those crooks in the morning."

CHAPTER FOURTEEN

TELEVISION INTERFERENCE

E veryone on board was dog tired. It was agreed to take the rest of the afternoon off to rest, so as to be able to start tracing out the trail to Cabrillo's grave with tomorrow's dawn.

"Why did they go in a zigzag, anyway?" Spud wanted to know. "They weren't trying to keep a secret from the Indians or something, were they?"

Dr. Bonilla answered, "The zigzag line, *muchacho,* is probably the path Cabrillo's sailors took in climbing the hillside to reach a location they were sure the elements would never destroy.

"I can picture it now—the pallbearers carefully measuring each leg of their melancholy journey up the hill, recording each change of direction by means of their ship's compass, so the exact site of the grave could be pinpointed afterward."

Tommy, who was beginning to feel the physical exhaustion brought on by his underwater expedition, headed for his quarters and stretched out on his bunk. He was dozing when Spud Kleveland, flushed from the excitement of the day's adventures, sought him out.

"I haven't had a chance to speak to you alone all day, Tommy," Spud greeted him, "but you're convinced now that we were wrong about Dr. Bonilla and Mr. Gerlock plotting to swindle my father, aren't you? The galleon and the lead chart convince you of that, don't they?"

"Anyone can make mistakes, Spud," Tommy yawned, and Spud left the stateroom without realizing that Tommy had not given him an answer to his questions.

For Tommy's part, the next thing he had to do was place a ship-to-shore radio call to Ross Jackson and tip him off about the day's developments, which were considerable.

It was Tommy's plan to visit the wheelhouse of the barge—a much larger room than its name implied, since it also housed the controls for all the *Triton IV's* loading and towing machinery—and place his radio call to the sheriff's office by means of Captain Tucker's rig.

This little scheme was nipped in the bud, however, when the group gathered in the messroom at dusk for a snack before retiring.

"The Kenyon Kid is challenging Phil Orr for the welterweight championship at eight tonight," Captain Tucker announced. "The fight's in Los Angeles and it's being televised on Channel Two, so you're all invited to the wheelhouse this evening. I've got a Channel Two Yagi mounted on the crane, and we get pretty fair reception out here."

Captain Tucker's television receiver, Tommy knew, was an ac-dc portable, and he was sorely tempted to ask if it could be brought down to the messroom where there was more seating available—until he recalled that the TV set was bolted to the bulkhead.

However, all was not lost. While everyone else was watching television, he could slip out unnoticed and send his radio message from Ed's launch. He knew that Ross Jackson would be expecting a report from him tonight, and the sheriff had no way of contacting the islands, except on schedule.

Everyone including Bonilla and Gerlock had accepted the Captain's invitation to watch the fights on the "idiot box," which meant Tommy would have to put in a token appearance, at least, or be conspicuous by his absence.

After their supper snack, he sought out Ed Morin, who had just made a trip ashore to padlock the radar hut "—just in case some vandals might be camping on the island and get to snooping around in my electronic equipment," Ed explained.

"Ed," Tommy asked his friend, "is it okay if I use your radio on the *Goose* tonight while the TV show's going on in the wheelhouse? I want to let Ross Jackson know the trap is ready to spring."

"You're welcome to use the rig, of course—but are you sure you've got all the evidence you need for an arrest?"

Tommy hesitated. "That propeller proves the galleon isn't the real McCoy—"

"Yes, but can you prove either Bonilla or Gerlock is aware of that propeller?"

Tommy rubbed the knot on his head. "Somebody slugged me and kicked me overboard to drown last night. Who else could it have been?"

Ed said gently, "Ross Jackson will say it could have been Cap'n Tucker, or me, or even Spud. You can't prove it wasn't accidental—you admitted that yourself."

Tommy had to admit that he was being overeager in his desire to see Gerlock and Bonilla arrested.

"Anyway," he said, "the sheriff's expecting a radio call from me this evening, and I want to know if he's had a cablegram from the real Dr. Bonilla in Spain. I'll never be convinced that the one you know isn't Lou Weber, Ed."

Ed chuckled and clapped Tommy on the back.

"Okay, Sherlock Holmes. Have your chat with the sheriff. But so far, I would say that Gerlock could cash those two checks for fifty thousand dollars without the law's being able to lay a finger on him."

A feeling of desperation came over Tommy when he returned to his bunk. He realized that he was alone with his terrible secrets, in a manner of speaking. Spud no longer shared his views about the two conspirators, and Ed's implacable logic seemed to indicate that he, too, was unconvinced that anything illegal was afoot.

At eight-thirty Tommy headed up to the wheelhouse. The entire complement of the expedition was there, watching Captain Tucker's "modulated milk bottle," as radio hams called a TV set.

They had tuned in "Eddie Abbott and his Barbarettes," a comedy show originating in Santa Bonita over KEYT, and were so engrossed in the comedian's antics that Tommy felt safe in slipping out to take care of his radio message.

Making his way aft to the starboard rope ladder which led down to the *Galloping Goose,* Tommy found that the weather had worsened with the setting of the sun. The moon and stars were obscured by a heavy, scudding overcast, and mammoth groundswells were rolling over the harbor bar to assault the *Triton IV,* making the barge wrench ominously against her four anchors.

It was no easy job for Tommy to transfer himself from the rope ladder to the bobbing cockpit of Ed Morin's launch, but he managed to make it safely into the cabin and switch on Ed's marine radio transceiver.

Up in the wheelhouse, Captain Tucker switched to Channel Two, Los Angeles, to pick up the nationally-televised prize fight at nine o'clock. His guests were still chuckling over the drolleries of the home talent show on Channel Three, and no one noticed Tommy's absence except Ed Morin, who knew where K6ATX was, and why.

When the nine o'clock commercial had run its interminable course, the network switched to ringside and the announcer lifted his voice to the assembled fans in the sports arena:

"Ladeeez an' gentlemen, in this corner, wearing white trunks, from Gambier, Ohio the challenger, the Kenyon Kid—"

At that moment the TV screen suddenly went blank and then was filled with heavy black herringbone patterns. Before Captain Tucker could cross the length of the wheelhouse to retune, a voice issued from the TV loudspeaker—a voice which everyone in the room recognized as Tommy Rockford's:

"KOU, KOU, KOU in San Pedro, this is the launch *Galloping Goose* at anchor in Cuyler Harbor, San Miguel Island, calling the marine operator at KOU and standing by. Come in please?"

Tommy's voice stopped. The television picture snapped back to normal, showing a brawny boxer in black trunks, champion Phil Orr, raising his gloved hands to acknowledge the ovation of the home town crowd.

"What in heck was Tommy's voice doing on TV?" Kurt Gerlock wanted to know, when another commercial came on the screen.

Captain Tucker explained, "He's making a ship-to-shore call on Ed's radio down in the launch, I guess. His signal's blocking the front end of my TV set because it's so close by."

Spud Kleveland, who was relaxing after the busiest day of his life, commented mysteriously "That's what we radio hams call 'Tennessee Valley Indians,' isn't it, Ed?"

Now it was Dr. Bonilla's turn to be puzzled.

"'Tennessee Valley Indians'? What on earth do you mean? Sometimes I think you Americanos never speak English anymore."

Spud, always glad to be explaining something to somebody, said "The initials of Tennessee Valley Indians also happen to be the initials of 'Television Interference,' which is the biggest bugaboo a radio ham has to bear."

"Hams can interfere with television?" Dr. Bonilla echoed. "Surely the ether is roomy enough for all!"

Spud chuckled ruefully. "Radio hams go to great pains to make sure their transmitters don't interfere with TV programs," he said, "but it seems we get the blame every time a passing taxicab radio or a defective neon sign or an electric razor hashes up a TV picture."

Ed Morin, who had headed the Santa Bonita ham club's TVI committee for several years, chimed in with his pet peeve: "The sad thing is that in ninety out of a hundred cases the fault lies with the TV receiver for not rejecting unwanted signals. But you can't tell a layman who's just paid five hundred dollars for a fancy mahogany TV set that the ham transmitter isn't at fault."

At that moment Tommy Rockford's voice once more came booming through the TV set's audio:

"KOU? This is Thomas H. Rockford Jr. aboard the launch *Galloping Goose*...that's right. Registered to Edward P. Morin...Yes. I want to place a person-to-person collect call to Sheriff Ross Jackson in Santa Bonita, ma'am...direct dial number 866-2720. If an assistant answers, tell them it's an emergency matter, and operator, please hook up the scrambler. Over."

The instant Tommy switched off his transmitter the TV picture came on again, showing the prize fighters sparring cautiously in the ring while the referee pranced around trying to keep out of the way.

"This is strange," Captain Tucker commented. "What kind of emergency would cause Tommy to radio the sheriff tonight?"

Across the darkened room, Ed Morin's face was white with tension. The next transmission Tommy made would be scrambled at the sheriff's end, but every word Tommy said would come booming out of Captain Tucker's speaker.

At all costs, Tommy had to be put off the air before he started talking about Bonilla and Gerlock.

Coming to his feet, Ed crossed over to the barge helm and reached up to grab the handle of the cord which operated the *Triton IV's* powerful air horn, used when navigating in heavy fogs.

The blast of that horn could be heard for miles, even if Tommy was wearing headphones down in the *Goose*.

Before Ed could yank the whistle cord, Tommy's voice issued from the TV set: "But listen, operator, this is a life or death matter. Try his home number. It's—"

Ed waited to hear no more. He jerked the foghorn cord to blast out the dots and dashes of six Morse code letters: Q-R-T—T-V-I.

The ear-splitting blast of the air horn on the roof over their heads nearly deafened the group in the wheelhouse. In ham language, QRT TVI meant *Stop sending—television interference.*

Would Tommy realize the signal was meant for him alone?

The radio transmitter down in the launch was still on, blocking the TV picture. But Ed had put his message through in time, for Tommy said hurriedly, "Please cancel the call, operator. I'll—place it later."

The radio carrier went off; the prizefight came on. The Kenyon Kid and the welterweight champion were still doing their ballet in midring.

Spud Kleveland let out a boyish cackle. "That's one way of getting rid of TVI. I wish it was that easy when the maid's sewing machine breaks up my Dodger baseball games at home."

Spud trailed off as he saw the look of consternation on his father's face. It suddenly occurred to the boy that no one was paying any attention to the TV fight.

"What did Tommy mean, a 'life or death matter'?" the newspaper publisher demanded, looking around. "I agree with the captain— why should Tommy be calling Sheriff Ross?"

Dr. Bonilla and Kurt Gerlock sat staring at the TV screen without seeing it. Their faces had turned ash-gray.

A thump of feet coming up the outside ladder reached their ears. Ed Morin said, "Here's Tommy now. He—he'll explain. He and Ross Jackson are close buddies, you know."

The wheelhouse door slid open and shut again, to admit Tommy.

"Was I—getting into the idiot box?" Tommy asked, his eyes seeking out Ed Morin.

"You were," Ed said, hoping against hope that Tommy could come up with an explanation which would allay the suspicions which must be churning in the brains of Gerlock and Bonilla. "I would say about two hundred dB over S-nine."

'Tommy," Chester Kleveland said sternly, "what's this 'life-or-death emergency' call you were placing to Ross's office?"

Tommy blushed. "I—I feel like an idiot," he said contritely. "You see—that is—when I left the house last night—to join you people at the wharf—"

"Yes—yes?" prompted Captain Tucker when Tommy faltered

into silence. He was aware that Gerlock and Bonilla were staring at him with eyes like gimlets.

"Speak up!" commanded Mr. Kleveland, angry now.

Out of nowhere came inspiration. "Well, I was afraid I'd forgotten to turn off the gas range at home. I wanted Ross Jackson to send a prowl car around to check."

For a moment Tommy's words hung on empty air. Then Mr. Kleveland and Captain Tucker relaxed and grinned.

"And I just remembered this very minute," Tommy went on in perfect truth, "that my folks are home now, so all my worry was for nothing."

Ed Morin chose that moment to shout, "Hey—the champ's down with a right hook to the jaw! Yay, Kenyon Kid!"

The tension of the moment was broken. The hassle on the TV screen took over everyone's attention. The champ, bleeding slightly on one lip, struggled gamely to his feet just as the bell ended a round.

Tommy took advantage of the action in the following round to slip out and retire to his own cabin.

He had been blocked in his attempt to radio Ross Jackson, but he couldn't be sure how suspicious Bonilla and Gerlock might be. What if he frightened the game away before the trap could close?

"I'd give anything in the world to be able to eavesdrop on that pair when they get back to their private cabin tonight to talk over this business," Tommy muttered to himself. "I'm convinced they're crooks, but as Ed said, I can't really prove a thing—"

And then he had an inspiration. Why not "bug" Gerlock's sleeping room tonight and listen in on what they said when they thought they were alone? For what better use could he put the pair of walkie-talkie sets he had brought along?

CHAPTER FIFTEEN

SPYING VIA HAM RADIO

Suiting action to thought, Tommy hauled one of his duffle bags out from under his bunk and rummaged inside. From it he took the two matching portable transceivers he had brought from home, in case they came in handy for intercom work during the expedition.

Each unit was a self-contained, battery-powered, radio transmitting and receiving station. Thanks to the miracle of miniaturization—transistors—and printed circuits instead of complicated wiring hookups, the case containing the transceiver was no larger than a pint milk carton. Tommy had built both units as a school science project.

The loudspeaker did double duty as a microphone when the "transmit" button was pushed. The antenna was a telescoping chromium tube which, when extended, measured eight feet—or one quarter of the wavelength on which the CBs were designed to operate.

Suddenly Tommy's enthusiasm tapered off—for reasons of ham radio ethics, rather than any technical problems involved. The latter did not exist, providing he could get inside Stateroom A and conceal one of the walkie-talkies to do the transmitting.

The ethical angle was something else again. The very idea of using radio for eavesdropping on private conversations was contrary to the high code of conduct by which conscientious radio amateurs had been operating for over half a century.

If he wanted to split hairs, Tommy could tell his conscience that he was using CB gear, not ham gear. The radios were limited in frequency range to the eleven-meter band only, for the use of Citizens' Banders who did not wish to take the technical examination required for a ham ticket. CB gear came in handy for intercom use such as this.

But now Tommy had to examine his own conscience. He was seriously considering planting a CBer's walkie-talkie in the captain's stateroom, switching it to send position, and using his other receiver to pick up whatever Bonilla and Gerlock said to each other in private.

There was also the matter of a minor violation of FCC regulations regarding leaving an unidentified radio transmitter on the air without an operator attending it. In this case, Tommy knew his quarter watt of power would preclude the transmission from traveling more than a mile or two from San Miguel Island—although freak atmospheric conditions might conceivably enable a listener several thousand miles away to copy the "skip."

"If police can tap a telephone wire to get evidence to convict criminals," Tommy finally decided, "I don't see anything wrong in using radio for spy purposes this once."

He slipped out of the bunk room into the raw, salt-laden wind which was scouring clouds of sand off the San Miguel slopes to sting his cheeks with its gritty barrage. They were in for a rough night tonight, even inside the harbor. Captain Tucker would be lucky if his anchors didn't drag and tomorrow found the *Triton IV* on the beach.

Tucking the small CB under his sweatshirt, Tommy headed up the ladder for a quick peek into the wheelhouse. The prize fight was now in its tenth round, and from the glimpse Tommy got of the screen, was as lackadaisical as ever with the Kenyon Kid and Phil Orr waltzing around in interminable clinches.

Breathing a silent prayer that the TV show would keep his intended "victims" occupied for at least another ten minutes, Tommy made his surreptitious way below and worked his way around the forward end of the deckhouse to reach Stateroom A, the captain's quarters.

He found the door unlocked. A moment later he slipped inside, his eyes narrowing against a glare of light from an unshaded bulb alongside the captain's shaving mirror.

Tommy glanced around quickly, trying to locate a spot where he could hide the radio gear. A radio the size of a pint milk container would be easy to conceal, but not an eight-foot whip antenna.

Also, he had to be sure the mouthpiece of the microphone was pointed toward the center of the room and was not too obstructed by other objects.

Suddenly Tommy burst out laughing. He had spotted the exact solution for his problem—a rack of fishing tackle in the corner nearest the double-deck bunk which Bonilla and Gerlock occupied.

Captain Tucker was an ardent fisherman, and because his barge was often anchored for weeks at a time at some isolated spot where oil-well exploration was going on, he had plenty of time to indulge his hobby, right from the deck of the *Triton IV*. As a result, he had a dozen or so fishing rods of varying types, together with reels.

Quickly crossing the room, Tommy squatted down and began pulling the telescoping radio antenna to its full ninety-six inch length. When the radio was placed on the deck at the bottom of the fishing tackle rack, the eleven-meter antenna looked like just another fancy fishing rod.

Remembering Poe's story of the purloined letter, the plot of which was based on the theory that the best place to hide an object was out in plain sight where it would actually escape notice, Tommy stepped back to the bunks to survey his handiwork.

The walkie-talkie with its dial and switches could not, of course, pass for a handle and spinning reel on a fishing rod. But by shifting a wickerwork creel a few inches to one side, Tommy could mask the radio set from view anywhere in the room, and still not impair the pick-up qualities of the sensitive crystal microphone.

"Acoustics should be perfect," Tommy muttered to himself, noting that Bonilla and Gerlock had closed the portholes against the bitter cold night wind. "They could even whisper and I'll bet this rig would copy every word."

He went back to the radio and switched it on, making sure the send-receive switch was in transmit position. There was a pilot bulb behind a ruby jewel on the front panel to indicate when the power was on, but it took only a minute to remove the light bulb from its socket.

"Now," Tommy chuckled, "if that pair of plotters don't have some pretty interesting things to say to each other after hearing me trying to call the sheriff via TVI tonight, I miss my guess."

Tommy slipped out of the stateroom and closed the door. Back in his own quarters he extended the antenna of the other CB radio and tuned to the transmitting frequency of the set in Stateroom A.

The microphone of the hidden transmitter picked up the ticking of a clock, the creak and groan of the barge lurching to the rough water, and the subdued noise of wind in a ventilator pipe.

He had done everything necessary to listen in on whatever occurred in Stateroom A after his two suspects retired from watching the TV prize fight...which might be very soon now.

Tommy telescoped the receiving antenna so as to conceal the second walkie-talkie under his bulky sweatshirt, and returned to the wheelhouse.

He doubted if anyone noticed his entrance, for he arrived just when the referee was counting out the Kenyon Kid in the fourteenth round.

"A lousy fight," commented their host, Captain Tucker, as he switched on the overhead lights. "Orr couldn't box a—a compass."

"Typical," complained Chester Kleveland, "of the tripe of entertainment television is foisting off on the public."

"Now Dad," chided young Spud mischievously, "are you sure you aren't sore at TV because they nibble at the advertising dollars you think belong to the newspapers?"

Kurt Gerlock chuckled, "That precocious kid of yours hit a raw nerve with that crack, didn't he?"

"Anyway," Captain Tucker said, "you're all welcome to stay and watch the movie on Channel Seven. It's going to be Charles Laughton in *Mutiny on the Bounty,* and you'll see San Miguel and the other Channel islands in a good many scenes, I understand."

Dr. Bonilla was mopping his face with a handkerchief.

"If you don't mind, Señores, I think I will retire," Dr. Bonilla said, flashing Gerlock what Tommy, watching closely, would have sworn was a "significant glance." "I very much fear I am getting seasick. Perhaps if I lie down—"

"I'll join you, Doc," Kurt Gerlock followed suit instantly. "We've got a busy day ahead of us tomorrow locating Cabrillo's bones, and I'm afraid we're in for a stormy night. We should have pitched camp on the island. At least it's stationary."

As Bonilla and Gerlock were preparing to leave, buttoning up their jackets against the expected blast of cold weather outside, Tommy drew Ed Morin aside and whispered, "I've planted a radio in their stateroom. Make some excuse to escort them to the door, won't you? I want to monitor whatever they talk about, once they think they're alone."

Ed Morin's eyes flashed with excitement. "Good boy, Tommy. Will do."

As Bonilla and Gerlock stepped out of the wheelhouse into the biting wind, Ed followed on their heels, making some remark about going to the engine room. When the three of them had disappeared down the companionway leading to the foredeck, Tommy turned to face the two Klevelands and Captain Tucker, who were apparently settling down to enjoy a rerun of an old movie which had been filmed near this very spot.

Stepping over to the TV set, Tommy snapped it off, then reached under his sweatshirt to take out his walkie-talkie.

"Tommy, what on earth's getting into you?" yelled Spud indignantly. "Turn that TV back on!"

Tommy was untelescoping the chrome antenna with the savage gesture of an angry knight unsheathing a sword for battle.

"Listen to me, all of you—especially you, Mr. Kleveland!" Tommy said crisply. "What I've got to tell you is the life-or-death matter I was planning to phone the sheriff tonight before Ed signaled me on the foghorn."

Chester Kleveland and the skipper exchanged puzzled glances. They could tell from Tommy's serious demeanor that he wasn't joking. Spud's face suddenly went pale as a fish's belly.

"I've got to talk fast," Tommy went on, "because we're all going to have our ears glued to this radio receiver just as soon as Dr. Bonilla and Kurt Gerlock reach their stateroom. You see," Tommy added, "I planted a hidden transmitter near their bunks. I want you all to hear whatever they have to say to each other when they think they're in private. I can almost guarantee it will come as a shock to you, their converstion."

Captain Tucker half rose from his chair. "Wait a minute, now!" he cried angrily. "You have no right to plant a microphone anywhere on board my—"

"I'm sorry, Captain," Tommy cut in sharply, "but I have good reason to believe that Dr. Bonilla, and possibly Kurt Gerlock, are criminals, out to rook Mr. Kleveland of one hundred thousand dollars. I planted that mike in their room to get my proof. All I ask is that you listen closely to this radio set I have here. It's tuned to the same frequency channel as the transmitter I concealed in Stateroom A a few minutes ago."

Chester Kleveland's face was a study in consternation. This was the first inkling he had had that anything was amiss where his guest Dr. Bonilla was concerned, and he obviously refused to believe any such monstrous nonsense now.

"Tommy, you trot right down there and bring that hidden mike to me, understand?" Kleveland thundered. "And apologize to my guests while you're about it! This is an outrage—"

It was his own son who put the cork on Kleveland's explosion.

"Dad, you'd better listen to what Tommy's trying to say. He—he has reason to be suspicious of Dr. Bonilla, all right."

At that moment a sound came from the tiny loudspeaker on the walkie-talkie in Tommy's hand. he turned the volume to maximum, and the sound became Kurt Gerlock's voice, with a door slamming in the background. Gerlock was saying, "Are you really getting queazy in the stomach, Lou, or just pretending?"

Dr. Bonilla's voice answered, but it no longer had the Spanish accent they were used to hearing. It sounded American—if anything, American with Brooklyn overtones:

"I'm a little seasick—but more than that, I'm beginning to get scared, Kurt. And stop calling me Lou—you might make a slip when it could do a lot of damage."

A long silence ensued, broken only by the sounds of footsteps in the cabin, and a sound of a man grunting with effort as he tugged off a garment.

"I've already had one hunch confirmed," Tommy Rockford whispered. "Gerlock calling Dr. Bonilla 'Lou.' It means he's really Lou Weber—a notorious swindler and con man—"

Tommy broke off as the loudspeaker came alive again:

"Whatcha mean you're beginning to get scared, Doc?" Gerlock wanted to know. "We've already collected fifty grand from Kleveland. What more d'ya want?"

Chester Kleveland's cheeks now turned as pale as Spud's.

"I want the whole hundred grand," Dr. Bonilla retorted, "and I don't want to have to go through the silly motions of digging up those bones you planted up on the plateau, either."

In the ensuing interval of silence, Tommy dropped some more blockbusters: "Cabrillo's bones will be counterfeit—just as the lead plate map was a counterfeit—and so was the *St. Regis* galleon. All

116

fakes. All part of a scheme to swindle you out of—"

Again voices issued from the rig in Tommy's hands, as broadcast by the hidden transmitter less than fifty feet away:

"That telephone call Tommy was making from the launch tonight," Bonilla rasped out. "Why should he want to report a life-or-death 'emergency' to the sheriff of the county? I tell you, Kurt, that kid found out something on that dive this afternoon that he isn't letting on. He's wise to us, I tell you! He's been suspicious of me from the very first, since he dropped that ham radio card with Bonilla's picture on it. We've been skating on thin ice ever since."

Gerlock, his voice sounding farther away from the hidden transmitter, answered thoughtfully. "I admit it gave me something to think about when Ed Morin jumped up and blew that foghorn to make Tommy stop talking. Otherwise we'd have heard whatever it was he aimed to telephone the sheriff, see?"

One thing about this conversation between the two conspirators had come as a surprise to Tommy: Dr. Bonilla, rather than Gerlock, was the leader of the pair. Only today he had believed that the aggressive Gerlock, rather than the self-effacing pseudo-Spaniard, was the brains behind the conspiracy.

"It's too bad," Bonilla went on angrily, "I didn't make sure young Rockford was dead before I dumped him over the side out in the Channel. I knew the minute he canceled a mountain climb to fly back to California that he must have caught on to Antonio Bonilla being a radio ham in Europe. That was the one weak chink in our armor, Kurt, that ham radio business."

Tommy tapped the bandaged knot on his head and whispered, "I've thought all day long that I was conked in the noggin and thrown overboard last night. I let you think it was an accident—but you heard what Bonilla just said."

"I wish," Gerlock's panicky voice issued from the CB radio speaker, "we could steal that launch and get out of here during the night. But with that storm that's blowing up, and both of us land-lubbers, we'd never make it to the mainland."

Gerlock's voice tapered out as he moved out of range of the hidden mike—Tommy made a quick guess that he had probably climbed into the upper bunk and turned his head into the blankets. But Bonilla's voice now came loud and clear, with a venomous malevolence which made his listeners' flesh creep, up in the wheelhouse:

"We've played this game long enough, Kurt. We know Kleveland's got that other fifty thousand dollar check in his wallet. It's as negotiable as a solid gold ingot at any bank we take it to. Kurt, I aim to get that check and scram out of here first thing tomorrow, understand? Providing the water's calm enough for Morin's launch to get out of the harbor with us."

Gerlock's voice seemed to come from a long distance away: "You mean—take the other check by force?"

"Why not? Why go on with this phoney hunt for a phoney skeleton? Where would we be if a sheriff's boat showed up to investigate Tommy's canceled radio call tonight? I say it's time we pushed the panic button and cleared out of here."

"We can't operate the launch," pointed out Gerlock.

"But Morin can—with a gun poking him in the ribs. Just as that stuffed shirt editor will fork over his wallet without giving me an argument."

Gerlock's frightened words came distinctly now: "Y-You won't kill anybody, Lou? I don't want no murder rap on this job—"

"If I kill anybody," Bonilla snapped, "it'll be the ham radio jerk who threw the monkey wrench in our whole operation—Rockford. Now turn out the light and shut up, Kurt. I got to rest. I've got a hard day ahead of me tomorrow."

CHAPTER SIXTEEN

CALAMITY IN THE GALLEY

E veryone jumped nervously as the bronze doorknob of the wheelhouse rattled and started to open. But it was Ed Morin who let himself in out of the storm, brows lifting to ask a silent question as he gestured toward the radio in Tommy's lap.

"Too late—show's over," said K6ATX. "But we picked up an earful."

Captain Tucker ground out a sailor's oath and said hoarsely, "An earful is right. Those two swabs down in my cabin are plotting to rob Mr. Kleveland of fifty thousand dollars tomorrow, commandeer you and your launch at gun's point, and maybe murder Tommy here before they escape!"

Ed gave a low whistle. "They've already had one pretty close crack at killing Tommy. What are we going to do about it, gentlemen?"

Tommy's jaw locked grimly as he strode past the wheel to the rack of electronic gear alongside the binnacle.

"I know what I'm going to do," he said crisply. "Complete my call to Ross Jackson and have him come over here and pick up those two homicidal maniacs tonight."

While Tommy was firing up the ship-shore radio telephone, Captain Tucker waggled his head pessimistically. "Sheriff might possibly fly over, but the way that norther is whippin' up the chop out on the channel, he sure won't make it in a police boat."

Chester Kleveland had not said a word. He sat in his chair, still staring at the blank television screen, wearing the haunted expression of a man caught in the toils of a nightmare from which he could not awaken.

Everyone went silent when KOU, the marine operator at San Pedro, answered Tommy's call from the *Triton IV*. This time, with no television interference to betray him, he got the call put through to the sheriff's office in a matter of moments. He recognized the deputy on duty as Barney Ontiveros, a long-time ham radio friend, W6FFF.

"Barney, this is K6ATX," Tommy said, "calling from the crane barge *Triton* IV over at Cuyler Harbor. When I called about an hour ago they said the sheriff was out. Has he come back yet?"

Ontiveros' voice issued from the speaker on the ceiling: "The sheriff's gone to Los Angeles, Tommy. He won't be back until sometime after midnight. Anything I can do for you? Walt Olson and Jimmy Webster and Ray Romero are sitting around here looking bored."

Tommy glanced at the group in the wheelhouse, holding the push-to-talk microphone close to his lips. He couldn't very well go into details over the air—there was no way of knowing who might be monitoring the frequency. Confederates of Lou Weber's, even...

"I may call back later tonight, pal," Tommy said. "Seventy three and out."

"Night, K6 Always Take X-lax. Be seeing you."

Tommy switched off the radio and turned to Captain Tucker with a question: "You have firearms aboard the *Triton*, haven't you?"

Tucker grinned bleakly. "A Winchester carbine I keep for pot-shooting at sharks, and my Navy 45 caliber automatic. But they're hanging from the wall in my cabin—waiting for those two crooks to arm themselves before they shave for breakfast."

Tommy's heart sank. "Does anyone else have a gun?"

The Klevelands shook their heads. Ed said lamely, "I always carry a rifle on the *Galloping Goose*, but this trip I left it at the shop to have a new 'scope installed."

Chester Kleveland seemed to come out of his trance for the first time in several minutes.

"If—if you knew I was being victimized by a couple of criminals, Tommy, why did you keep it a secret from me?"

Tommy said gently, "Sir, I didn't want to alarm you unnecessarily until I had some proof to offer you. The reason I flew down from Washington State Sunday was because I suspected Dr. Bonilla might be an impostor, but I had no real proof of it—and no proof at all that Kurt Gerlock was a criminal.''

Kleveland's shoulders lifted and fell in a heavy sigh.

"Did I understand you to say, Tommy, that both the galleon and the lead plate were—counterfeit?''

"I'm afraid so, sir. Phoney just like the bones of Cabrillo, if we went through the motions of digging them up. Gerlock must have visited San Miguel secretly and buried a human skeleton of some kind, but—''

"Suppose,'' interrupted Mr. Kleveland, "you start from the beginning and brief me in on this business. It is utterly beyond my comprehension that anything as convincing as that Spanish galleon Ed found with the RUM this morning could be faked.''

Tommy said, "I confess that mystery has me stumped, sir, but when I finish my story, you'll know that that galleon we explored today wasn't the *St. Regis* of four centuries ago.

"To begin with, a few days before Spud telephoned to invite me to join this expedition, I had had a DX contact with a ham named Antonio Bonilla, EA7WK, in Seville, Spain...''

During the twenty minutes it took Tommy Rockford to tell his story, winding up with his startling discovery of a modern propeller attached to the sternpost of the supposed sixteenth century galleon outside Sombrero Rock, the storm outside had increased to a point where Captain Tucker found it expedient to go out and double-check the four anchors he had out.

When he returned to the two boys and two men in the pilot house a few minutes later, it was with the disturbing news that he had tried the knob of the door of Stateroom A and found it bolted on the inside.

"I gave Dr. Bonilla—or Lou Weber, whatever his real monicker is—the only key to the cabin that I happen to have on board,'' Tucker concluded, "which sort of puts the kibosh on our locking them up until the sheriff can get here. With them having the only guns on board, it sort of gives them all the high cards in this game, don't it?''

Tommy had been pacing the floor of the wheelhouse like a caged tiger, cudgeling his brains for some solution to their desperate dilemma. Something had to be done to prevent the two criminals from killing somebody early tomorrow morning, in case they got panicky about making their escape.

"Mr. Kleveland,'' Tommy said finally, "We've got to play to

their weakness, which is greed. If Dr. Bonilla thought it would cost him money if he brought this thing into the open by robbing you at gun's point, he wouldn't make his play, would he?''

Chester Kleveland looked puzzled. ''Just what are you getting at, Tommy? I'll confess this situation has completely bewildered my thinking powers at the moment. I just can't believe I could be played for such a sucker.''

Tommy said, ''Bright and early tomorrow, announce that you're so sure we'll find Cabrillo's bones that you're willing to raise the ante. Tell Bonilla that if you actually see the skeleton, and he as an authority on Cabrillo can identify it as Cabrillo's, that you'll pay Kurt Gerlock one hundred thousand dollars—twice the amount of the certified check you're holding in your wallet.''

Ed Morin's face lighted up. ''Tommy's got something there, sir. It'll take time tracking down the fake directions to find the grave—and also give time for the sheriff to get here after he returns from Los Angeles tonight.''

The meeting in the wheelhouse broke up on that note. They would use the promise of an extra $50,000 bonus to keep Gerlock and Bonilla from doing anything desperate.

Back in Stateroom 2 with Spud, Tommy crawled into his sleeping bag and tried to sleep, but sleep would not come.

His mind kept wrestling with the puzzle of the Spanish galleon he and Gerlock had explored today. Tommy believed he knew the answer to that mystery—why a sixteenth-century galleon should be equipped with a modern propeller—but in order to prove his theory, he needed to do some research in the back files of the *News-Star*.

The immediate problem was to devise some scheme whereby he could get back to Santa Bonita tomorrow without rousing the suspicions of Bonilla and Gerlock.

After a long period of tossing and turning, the answer finally came to Tommy. His plan involved a desperate gamble with Cabrillo's lead plate map, now reposing in the pantry of the galley, but if it worked, it would mean that Mr. Kleveland would send him to town on a legitimate errand.

Having formulated a plan, K6ATX's nerves relaxed. He closed his eyes and was almost instantly asleep.

The squall blew itself out during the hours immediately after midnight, and when daybreak came to San Miguel Island on Wednesday, the sun shown in an enamel-blue sky and the waters of Santa Barbara Channel as far as Point Concepcion were as smooth as a millpond.

It was a haggard-looking group that assembled in the messroom with the first pink break of dawn. Early as the skipper had arisen, Tommy had beaten him to the galley; he had the messroom filled with the heady aroma of coffee and sizzling bacon before Ed Morin and the two Klevelands entered with the captain.

A feeling of unbearable tension congealed the messroom when Kurt Gerlock and Lou Weber, alias Antonio Bonilla, put in their appearance a few minutes later.

The two conspirators iooked drawn and grim, but so, for that matter, did everyone else aboard the *Triton IV*. Spud had had a bout with seasickness during the night, and from the looks of Bonilla's gray cheeks, so had he.

Both of the swindlers had their fists thrust into the pockets of their heavy jackets, and there was no doubt in anyone's mind that two of those pockets contained automatic pistols.

"Kurt," sang out Chester Kleveland, "I've got some news for you—mighty good news." He raised his voice to call out, "Tommy, leave your cooking chores for a minute and listen to this. I want everybody to hear what I have to tell our friend Mr. Gerlock."

Gerlock flicked a suspicious glance at Bonilla, knots of muscle gritting at the hinges of his jaws. Bonilla seemed to mutter something under his breath to reassure Gerlock, for he said surlily, "Fetch me a cup of java, Spud. I can listen to good news with a stomach full of hot coffee a lot better than empty."

Spud Kleveland jumped to do Gerlock's bidding, vanishing into the galley after the coffee pot. During the night quite a few dishes had come unstowed, resulting in a cleaning up job for Tommy before he could get breakfast started.

"Okay, boss," Gerlock said, seating himself on a bench opposite the *News-Star* publisher. "What's the good news?"

Under the table, Chester Kleveland could almost see Gerlock training the blued barrel of a .45 automatic in his direction. He struggled to keep his voice steady and controlled:

"I'm so convinced that we will have found Cabrillo's grave before the sun sets today," Kleveland said, "that I am going to back my optimism with deeds rather than words."

As he spoke, Kleveland removed his wallet from his pocket and from it, a green-tinted treasurer's check which everyone in the messroom knew was his certified draft for $50,000, made out in Kurt Gerlock's name.

Gerlock was already starting to reach for the check when without warning, Kleveland ripped it in two lengthwise and, as Gerlock stared in horror, shredded it into bits.

"My fifty thousand G's!" howled Gerlock, lapsing into underworld slang for the first time. "What in—"

He broke off as Kleveland lifted a reassuring hand.

"I'm so sure we're going to find Cabrillo's grave," the Santa Bonita publisher said, "and so sure Dr. Bonilla will be able to identify it as authentic, that I am going to replace this fifty thousand dollar draft with one for one hundred thousand dollars, payable to both of you. And if Dr. Bonilla's professional ethics keep him from accepting rewards—and in no way do I intend this gesture to sound like a bribe, my good Doctor—then the entire one hundred thousand dollars goes to you, Mr. Gerlock!"

Before Gerlock had time to react, Spud Kleveland gave a blood-curdling shriek from the galley pantry, where he had gone to get a coffee cup.

Of one accord the others rushed through the galley and massed at the pantry door, fully expecting to see that young Spud had either cut himself on a knife or had spilled scalding coffee all over himself.

Instead, Spud was pointing at the large enameled pan on the pantry table, where Mr. Kleveland had photographed the Cabrillo map yesterday afternoon.

Lying upside down in the pan was the pantry's hot plate which Bonilla had used to heat water for cleaning the lead map. The electric cord still connected the hot plate to a wall socket supplying 120 volts ac from the barge's electrical system.

The hot plate was on, and smoke was wisping up from the pan, filling the pantry with a strange, toxic odor. The pan seemed to contain liquid quicksilver.

"Our Cabrillo map!" Spud finally managed to choke out. "It's—*it's been melted!*"

For a long moment a stunned silence prevailed. Then Captain Tucker muttered, "The hot plate must've slid off the shelf and landed upside down in the pan during the storm last night—"

Everyone was too busy staring at the puddle of liquid lead to see the triumphant glint that flickered in Tommy's eyes.

CHAPTER SEVENTEEN

SECRET ORDERS FOR SPUD

For a moment Tommy thought Chester Kleveland was going to keel over in a faint. But it was Gerlock who seemed most dismayed by Spud's discovery of the ruined chart.

"This means we'll never locate Cabrillo's skeleton!" Gerlock shouted. "Even if the Navy let us dig on the island the rest of our lives!" He wheeled savagely on Bonilla. "You stupid idiot, this wouldn't have happened if you'd pulled the plug on that electric plate last night!"

Doc Bonilla, taken aback by the ferocity of his partner, choked out, "But I—I'm positive I did switch off the electricity yesterday—"

It was Chester Kleveland who then remembered the obvious solution to their difficulties.

"Calm down, everybody!" the editor said, his voice breaking on a nervous giggle. "Are you folks forgetting I took several close-up photographs of that map?"

The relief that greeted Kleveland's news was almost ludicrous to see. Then Gerlock, always the pessimist, came up with a joy-killer.

"You'll have to get the films developed first. We don't have to have a positive print on paper; we can use the negative—but do we have a darkroom aboard?"

Captain Tucker shook his head. "Few crane barges in the oil business come equipped with photographic labs, Mr. Gerlock."

The liquified lead in the enameled pan was giving off toxic fumes which drove everyone back into the galley. Spud tarried to jerk the electric plug from the socket and then slid the tray along the table to the sink. When he turned the faucet on he narrowly escaped being sprayed with molten lead droplets as the hot metal practically exploded with a hissing burst of steam.

Back in the open messroom, Kurt Gerlock said "Where's the nearest darkroom where we can develop those films? Town?"

Kleveland nodded. "I'm afraid so. We'll have to send them back to the photo lab at Santa Bonita by Ed Morin's launch. I can have them returned in my *News-Star* helicopter, of course, but even so we can't get the search underway before one o'clock this afternoon, at the earliest."

Gerlock thought that over for a moment and said, "Well, we got all day Thursday to work, before the Navy missiles start plowing up the island. I think we can cut 'er, time-wise."

Bonilla said with a note of sarcasm meant for his partner alone, "With a hundred thousand dollars waiting in that grave, we can do some mighty fast map-reading, eh, amigo?"

At that moment Chester Kleveland chanced to catch Tommy's eye and saw K6ATX wink and point to himself.

"The time won't be wasted," Tommy said. "You wanted photographs taken of the wrecked galleon, Mr. Kleveland, and I can do that with my underwater Leica, during the day."

Gerlock, who had been sitting with his back to Tommy, whirled around on the bench and protested, "I'd better handle that photo detail, son. Underwater photography is my profession."

Tommy thought, "You're worried for fear I'd take a photograph of that propeller, aren't you? And maybe even the marine engine inside the hull." Aloud, he answered Gerlock and at the same time put an idea into Mr. Kleveland's head:

"You're right, sir. In that case maybe Ed had better stay on the island to operate the RUM—you'll need all the extra floodlighting you can get, down at the wreck of the *St. Regis*—and that'll leave me free to operate the *Galloping Goose* and rush the film back to town for processing."

Mr. Kleveland nodded in approval of Tommy's plan. "And while Tommy's getting the negatives developed at the *News-Star* lab, Spud can drop in at the bank and get a certified check drawn in Mr. Gerlock's name in the amount of one hundred thousand dollars. Unless," Kleveland said, "you'd just as soon wait until Friday to pick up your money at the bank. For purposes of dramatizing the thing, I had sort of visualized getting a picture of you standing beside Cabrillo's grave, possibly with the skeleton showing in the picture, while I handed you the check with Dr. Bonilla looking on."

Spud broke in with a protest: "I don't want to leave the island, Dad. You go to town with Tommy and get the check, then come back on the helicopter and Tommy can bring the launch back."

Kleveland said, "I want to direct the underwater photography by way of Ed's TV screen. Right now, Spud, what this meeting needs is some good hot coffee. Hustle it up!"

While Tommy and Spud acted as waiters to serve the hot breakfast which Tommy had already prepared prior to the interruption over the destroyed lead plate, Captain Tucker absented himself from the messroom.

When he returned, the captain took occasion to visit the galley long enough to pass along some ominous news to Tommy:

"I slipped into the stateroom to recover that CB radio set you left among my fishing rods," Tucker whispered, "and I found out that the clip was gone from my forty-five Colt and the bolt is missing from the Winchester rifle."

"They've made sure our side won't use your guns, then."

"Sure. They gave the clip and the bolt the deep six, I imagine—tossed 'em overboard."

In the act of returning to the messroom with another cup of coffee, Captain Tucker turned back to Tommy, a quizzical expression on his face. He jerked a thumb in the direction of the pantry.

"You set that hot plate on top of the lead chart? You melted it deliberately?"

Tommy nodded and winked. "Sure. It had no value as an historical relic anyway. And it did set things up so Mr. Kleveland has a logical reason for sending me back to town to get his films developed."

Tucker stifled a chuckle of appreciation. "Tommy, you dog, you! A person would have to get up pretty early to outsmart you."

"I had to get up pretty early," Tommy conceded, "to turn on that hot plate before anybody was up."

Breakfast was over by seven o'clock. Gerlock was the first to leave the table, mumbling something about rowing ashore in the barge dinghy as soon as he got into his diving suit. Dr. Bonilla followed him shortly.

Tommy, removing dishes from the messroom to the galley so that Spud could perform KP duty on them, carefully set aside the thick china cups Gerlock and Bonilla had used, placing them in paper sacks which he was careful to label.

Spud, spotting this activity, raised an inquiring eyebrow.

"The sheriff will be glad to get fingerprints for those two characters," Tommy explained. "That way, if Dr. Bonilla is really Lou Weber, the FBI's fingerprint files should be able to prove it in a hurry."

When Tommy went out on deck it was to find that Ed Morin had already taken Gerlock and Dr. Bonilla ashore. He could hear Ed trying to get the RUM's generator started, out behind the radar hut.

While Tommy was warming up the engine of the *Galloping Goose* for the two-hour speed run to Santa Bonita, Mr. Kleveland and Spud came aboard with leather cases filled with the numerous camera film holders containing the exposed film Tommy was to deliver to the darkroom technician at the *News-Star*.

"Dad," complained Spud, "I still think you should go to the bank instead of me. I'm supposed to be a newspaper reporter, not an errand boy—"

"Son," Kleveland said, "you aren't going to bring back any one hundred thousand dollar check. Can't you see that's just a stall to keep Bonilla and Gerlock from doing anything rash? Your real job is to get those films back here by helicopter this afternoon—and Tommy's is to locate the sheriff or a deputy and bring him back here to arrest those two swindlers."

Just before going back aboard the *Triton IV*, Chester Kleveland slipped Tommy a sealed envelope on which was scrawled, *Secret Orders. Open after you are at se*a.

A few moments later Tommy was circling the barge and sending the swift *Galloping Goose* through the narrow inlet of the Devil's Jaw. Not until he was a mile from San Miguel did Tommy slit open the envelope to read Mr. Kleveland's orders:

Don't bring Spud back with you. I'm afraid Gerlock and Bonilla may resist arrest and I don't want Spud put in danger. I know this will break his heart so I'm passing the buck to you to break the bad news. C.H.K.

CHAPTER EIGHTEEN

CLUE FROM THE MORGUE

Tommy had promised Spud he could steer the *Galloping Goose* once they were clear of the shoals outside the Devil's Jaw. The boy came into the cabin just in time to see Tommy put something into his pocket.

"That's the note Dad slipped you," Spud said matter-of-factly. "He's told you not to let me come back."

Tommy hesitated, knowing that Spud's heart and soul were in this adventure—not only for the thrills, but because he was launching his own journalistic career with the story he would be writing for the *News-Star*.

"You know how fathers are," Tommy said gently. "You can bet my folks wouldn't let me go back to San Miguel if they knew I was in town."

A big fat tear rolled out from under Spud's horn-rimmed glasses and coursed down his cheek.

"This whole thing has been hoodooed," the boy said. "First Dr. Bonilla turns out to be a phoney. And then the galleon turns out to be a replica with a propeller on it. And instead of finding Cabrillo's grave, that mystery is as unsolved as it ever was."

Tommy turned the wheel over to his younger friend and said "Spud, I'm ashamed of you. I don't pretend to be a newspaperman, but I can see a lot more drama and newsworthiness in capturing an international confidence man and his crooked accomplice than if everything had buzzed along on an even keel."

Spud, his attention centered on the novelty of piloting a speed-boat for the first time in his life, brightened perceptibly.

"You know, Tommy, I hadn't looked at it from that angle. Why sure—the way things turned out, maybe I've got an even bigger story. The mystery of how that galleon got there at Sombrero Rock is almost as intriguing as the mystery of where the Spaniards buried Cabrillo."

Tommy grinned enigmatically. "I've been giving that phoney galleon a lot of thought," he said, "and I think I know the answer. All I need is proof—and I expect to find that when we get to town this morning."

Spud was overcome with curiosity.

"Where? How? What's your theory, Tommy?"

Tommy switched on the marine radiotelephone. "I think I can find the clues we need to solve that galleon mystery," he said, "buried in the files of your dad's newspaper."

Spud looked incredulous. "You won't find any galleon shipwreck written up in the *News-Star*, for gosh sakes!" the boy protested. "Our files go back a little over a hundred years, but that galleon is older than that, surely."

Tommy switched to the ship-shore channel and called KOU, the marine operator at San Pedro, with whom he placed a station-to-station call to the Santa Bonita *News-Star*, Extension 500—which was Chester Kleveland's office.

A few moments later Tommy heard the voice of Penny Harts, Mr. Kleveland's private secretary.

"Penny," Tommy said, "have a car down at the wharf to pick up some passengers of Mr. Kleveland's around ten o'clock, will you please?"

"Yes suh, will do," Penny said in her cheerful Southern drawl. Then, doing a mental double-take, Mr. Kleveland's secretary said, "Tommy Rockford! I'd know your voice anywhere! Listen! You're not calling long distance from the State of Washington, are you?"

Tommy laughed. "No, I'm not calling from a mountain peak, Penny. As a matter of fact, I'm out in the Channel opposite Gaviota Pass, telephoning from a friend's cabin cruiser. Penny, do you have a key to the older files of the *News-Star*—the ones they keep up in the tower?"

"I have a master key that unlocks anything in the building, yes. But if you want to get into the archives vault, you'll have to have written permission from the boss, and he's out of town."

Tommy said, "Will verbal permission from the boss's son get me in there? This is official business for Mr. Kleveland."

Penny replied, "Spud's say-so will open any door in the place, Tommy. Got to keep in good with that little darling. You know—he may be my boss someday."

Tommy terminated the call at that point. Penny Harts, of course unaware that her voice was issuing from a loudspeaker to which Spud was listening, had said exactly the right thing. Spud now realized that he was a key man in this shore expedition. As the boss's son, he was responsible for getting Tommy into the newspaper files where, if Tommy's hunch proved correct, he would solve the riddle of the phantom galleon off Sombrero Rock...

At ten o'clock sharp, Tommy nosed the *Galloping Goose* into a mooring slip alongside Stearn's Wharf and he and Spud carried the boxes of undeveloped photo film up the ramp to where Paul Bevlen, Mr. Kleveland's helicopter pilot and part-time chauffeur, was waiting for them in a *News-Star* sedan.

Within five minutes Bevlen was letting them off at the city plaza in front of the *News-Star* building. Here the boys separated, Spud hurrying to the photographic lab to get his father's San Miguel films developed posthaste, Tommy making a beeline for Mr. Kleveland's office.

"Spud will be along in a few minutes, Penny," Tommy told Mr. Kleveland's pretty redheaded secretary, who was studying for her Novice Class ham ticket this summer. "I'm working inside a pretty tight schedule, though, so if you could let me into the morgue right away..."

Penny, Tommy could see, was consumed with curiosity over what was going on, but her professional training forbade her asking too many questions.

"You'll find Georgia filing clips in the morgue," Penny said, "and she'll let you into the tower archives where the old stuff is kept—providing you can convince her you've got any business in there."

Tommy took an elevator to the third floor of the tower and found himself in the newspaper's library, or morgue. Luckily for him, Georgia Sheftic, the librarian, had been a friend of his mother's since long before Tommy was born.

"Georgia, I want to see the latest copy of the *Hollywood Mo-*

tion Picture Almanac, may I?''

Almost before he had finished speaking Mrs. Sheftic had the requested volume off her library shelf. It was a dictionary-sized tome which listed every producer, cameraman, director, actor, technician, press agent and what have you in the entire motion picture and television industry.

''This one's nineteen eighty, but it's the latest we've got,'' the librarian said. ''Don't tell me you think you're handsome enough to go into the movies!''

''No''—Tommy went along with the gag—''this is a technical matter. I've invented a way to take the sound out of movies. It'll revolutionize the industry.''

Mrs. Sheftic clucked her tongue with feigned amazement.

''Silent pictures!'' she said in awe-struck tones. ''What you electronic geniuses won't think of next—''

Tommy's hands trembled with eagerness as he leafed through the big book until he came to the Gs. He was looking for the biographical data on one Kurt Gerlock, veteran movie cameraman.

Spud Kleveland came drifting into the library from the photo lab, to find Tommy over at a table, running his finger down a column of fine print under the listing *Gerlock, Kurtis, cameraman, producer.*

''What's happening?'' Spud inquired.

''This is a Who's Who in Hollywood kind of almanac, Spud,'' Tommy explained. ''I'm checking on all the motion pictures that Kurt Gerlock was ever connected with.''

Spud scowled in bewilderment. He was still in a melancholy mood over his father's refusal to let him come back to San Miguel for the climax of their adventure.

''Who cares?''

''You'll care, if my hunch works out...Here it is!'' Tommy exclaimed, his voice rising on a note of excitement. ''In 1953 Kurt Gerlock was chief cameraman for a movie called *Pirates of the Spanish Main.* I faintly remember seeing a rerun of it on the late late show a few years back on TV—''

Spud took off his glasses and polished them absently. He knew that Gerlock had worked in hundreds of movies in his long career behind the viewfinder, so why was Tommy so excited about a pirate picture filmed before both of them were born?

''And now,'' Tommy said, opening the almanac to the index,

"we'll look up what it has to say about a movie named *Pirates of the Spanish Main*. I think, Spud, we'll come up with some very interesting information."

Spud was still too engrossed in his blue mood to work up any enthusiasm as he saw Tommy looking up the data on the movie Gerlock had made in 1953.

"Ah, here it is," Tommy said exultantly. "*Pirates of the Spanish Main*. Low-budget B picture. I'll skip the names of the director and cast and stuff...Listen, Spud:

> "*Pirates was shot in 38 days and brought in under budget. Marine exteriors shot off Channel Islands, simulating Caribbean area; interiors at Flying A studios, Hollywood. This picture was notable for industry's extensive use of underwater cinematography on ocean bottom instead of in studio tank, using camera and submarine techniques pioneered by K. Gerlock, chief cameraman.*"

Tommy looked up, his face shining with excitement. Spud still looked blank.

"You still don't get it, do you?" he accused WA6IBR. "Gerlock filmed a pirate movie off the Channel Islands—and San Miguel is one of the Channel Islands. And what kind of ships would be in a movie about the Spanish Main?"

Spud's jaw sagged open. "Galleons!"

"Of course! My hunch is that the galleon we found out at San Miguel is not the *St. Regis* of four hundred years ago, but a movie prop that Gerlock had burned and sunk while he was shooting *Pirates of the Spanish Main* in 1953!"

The boys' next objective was the *News-Star* files for the year 1953. A few minutes later Georgia Sheftic had ushered them into the musty-smelling archives vault in the bell tower, where a century's file of the *News-Star* and its pioneer predecessors was kept for research purposes.

The 1953 volume was a ponderous thing weighing forty-odd pounds, yellowed with age, its top layered with the dust of decades.

"What are we looking for now, Tommy?" Spud wanted to know.

"The papers used to write up the movie companies working in the Santa Bonita area," Tommy said. "I imagine the actors and actresses who worked in *Pirates of the Spanish Main* over on the islands were put up here in town."

Beginning with January, 1953, Tommy began to skim through the bound volume of newspapers. He was halfway through the month of May when the boys spotted what they had been searching for—a five-column photograph showing a high-pooped Spanish galleon, smoke billowing from a fire amidships

In the background, half obscured by ˌmoke and flames, loomed the hazy outlines of a rock shaped like a Mexican sombrero. And if that was not identification enough, the caption told them this was the motion picture version of the galleon *St. Regis*:

FULL-SIZE REPLICA OF ANCIENT SPANISH GALLEON
WRECKED OFF SAN MIGUEL HARBOR BY MOVIEMAKERS

The newspaper story accompanying the picture consummated Tommy's successful "detective work." Spud peered over his shoulder as Tommy read the article aloud, for Spud's vision was not good enough for fine print in a dimly lighted room:

ON LOCATION, SAN MIGUEL IS., MAY 14 (Special to News-Star*)—Dozens of radio messages from fishing boats and passenger steamers have been received by the Coast Guard, reporting "a large sailing vessel in flames off Cuyler Harbor, San Miguel Island."*

In each case the Coast Guard voiced their thanks, but stated that the burning ship was deliberately set afire by her owners, as part of the making of a motion picture, "Pirates of the Spanish Main," directed by Saul Winestein for Flying A Productions.

A full-sized replica of a Sixteenth Century galleon was built at an Oakland shipyard last winter, complete with carved plaster dragons on the poop, and simulated metal fittings such as cannon, chains, capstans and anchors made of wood painted to resemble metal. The ship was copied from ancient Spanish etchings and marine records.

In the climax of the picture, supposedly filmed off the Yucatan Peninsula in the Caribbean, the galleon, set afire by buccaneers, was permitted to drift against Sombrero Rock at the mouth of Cuyler Harbor.

The spectacular fire and internal explosions were recorded by a battery of motion picture cameras mounted on a barge anchored nearby. After the galleon had sunk in sixty feet of water, chief cameraman Kurt Gerlock donned a diver's suit and, equipped with underwater lights and a waterproof camera, took considerable footage on the ocean bottom.

Although the galleon appeared to be powered by its sails alone, it actually was propelled by an inboard engine cunningly concealed from the cameras even during close-up scenes filmed on board.

Director Winestein has promised the News-Star *to ask his studio to have the world premiere of "Pirates of the Spanish Main" at the Granada Theater in Santa Bonita early next spring. Included in the cast are several extras recruited from our city.*

When Tommy had finished reading the old newspaper account, he and Spud sat in mute contemplation for several minutes.

"It all fits together like a jigsaw puzzle, doesn't it?" Spud finally broke the silence. "Gerlock had sunk the hulk in 1953, so he knew it was probably there now. So it was easy to dive down and plant that fake lead plate in the skipper's cabin, just like you found it ..."

Tommy shuddered, remembering something. "When I turned on that electric hot plate this morning in the galley of the *Triton IV*, it was with misgivings," he admitted. "What if I *had* destroyed a genuine relic from 1581? It sure looked convincing."

Spud's eyes shone with hero-worship as he followed K6ATX out of the archives room.

"To think all of this started with a DX conversation with the real Dr. Bonilla in Spain," Spud said pensively. "By the way, I wonder if he flew over from Seville?"

When they were alone in the privacy of the automatic elevator again, Tommy said, "I'm going over to the sheriff's office next, to see if they got a cablegram from EA7WK. Could be the real Dr. Bonilla is waiting for news. So far as he knows, I'm still up in W7-land. I hadn't decided to fly home when the QRM took out our QSO."

Spud said wistfully, "I've got to stick around and give the photo prints to Mr. Bevlen to fly back to the island." Tears welled in his eyes. "There's not much chance for me to stow away on a helicopter, even if Mr. Bevlen would let me. Just a big plexiglass bubble with a windmill over it."

Back on the street, Tommy instructed his sorrowing pal, "Tell Bevlen to tell Ed Morin that I'll bring the *Galloping Goose* back to the island this afternoon. The sheriff wouldn't have room for me in his helicopter either."

Over a solemn handshake the two boys parted company, each happily unaware that the real dangers of their adventure were yet to come.

CHAPTER NINETEEN

TERROR ON THE TRITON IV

Arriving at the courthouse, Tommy went straight to the sheriff's office in the jail wing, where he found Deputy Ontiveros on duty as usual.

"Ross back from LA yet?" Tommy inquired.

"Just talked to him on the radio," W6FFF replied, "and he's flying back tomorrow morning, early. He's meeting a guy at the International Airport just before midnight."

Disappointment stabbed through K6ATX. Mr. Kleveland and the others were depending on him to bring the sheriff back to San Miguel this afternoon to take Bonilla and Gerlock into custody.

"That means he won't be back to Santa Bonita for another couple of hours, assuming he doesn't dawdle along the way and doesn't run into any freeway traffic."

Barnie Ontiveros chuckled. "Freeway traffic won't slow Ross down this trip, Tommy. He took the chopper. Only takes about thirty minutes to get up here in a whirlybird."

That the sheriff was flying back by helicopter was at least good news, for he could be contacted en route by radio and change course directly to San Miguel Island. The Navy had an airstrip for conventional planes on the plateau above Cuyler Harbor, but the helicopter could land on the beach at low tide.

"Any chance of calling him back," Tommy said, "and letting me yak with him? I have some rather urgent business to discuss with Ross. Sheriff's business."

Ontiveros shook his head. Before he could explain, he took time off to answer a query from some radio prowl car in a remote corner of Santa Barbara County. Having a territory as large as the entire State of Delaware to patrol, Ross Jackson had pioneered in the use of electronics and computers in law enforcement.

Official traffic disposed of, W6FFF turned back to Tommy, who was placing two paper sacks on the counter in front of him.

"Sorry about Ross," he said, "but with a whole day to kill, he's picking up his nephew in Pasadena and taking him out to Disneyland, so he's out of touch by radio, I'm afraid. What's in the paper bags, kid?"

Tommy said, "A couple of coffee cups well plastered with fingerprints, I hope. The sheriff will want an FBI report on 'em."

Ontiveros thumbed an intercom switch. When a voice from somewhere else in the building said hollowly, "Identification Bureau," Ontiveros said, "Fingerprint job."

Tommy relaxed. He knew the speed and efficiency with which Jackson's experts would lift the fingerprints off the stoneware cups, photograph them, and send them via facsimile to the Federal Bureau of Investigation for checking. Before the day was over, thanks to the magic of computer automation, Sheriff Jackson would know whether Gerlock and Bonilla had police records anywhere in the world.

"By the way," Tommy said, "has Ross received a cablegram from Seville, Spain, in the last couple of days?"

"From EA7WK, Tony Bonilla?" Ontiveros said. "Sure. Asking the sheriff to meet him at the airport tonight. Tony flew all the way from Lisbon on some deal you cooked up."

"You mean Dr. Bonilla's the person Ross is picking up at the International Airport tonight?"

"Nobody else. I'm looking forward to meeting Tony. I've had jillions of single sideband QSOs with him."

A courier from the fingerprint division arrived to pick up Tommy's paper sacks. "I marked them B and G for identification," Tommy explained. "That's all you'll need—I don't have time to go into details."

He turned to W6FFF. "Mind if I borrow the sheriff's word processor to leave him a sort of report?"

"Help yourself."

In the privacy of the sheriff's office, Tommy rattled off a detailed account of what had transpired out on San Miguel Island, together with his own narrow escape from drowning Monday night, the incriminating information which his walkie-talkie had picked up in Gerlock's stateroom on Tuesday night, and the revelation which the 1953 files of the *News-Star* had given him proving Gerlock's phantom galleon to be a movie prop.

He wound up with, *We'll be playing along with Gerlock's make-believe hunt for Cabrillo's grave Thursday morning. Sooner you can get over to San Miguel the better. Remember we have to evacuate the island by sundown tomorrow or get clobbered by Navy missiles.*

Hoping against hope that no one would tell his father and mother that they had seen him in town today—so far as the Rockfords knew, their son was up in Washington with the Sierra Clubbers—Tommy bummed a ride from one of the sheriff's prowl cars and returned to the wharf.

While he was gassing up the *Galloping Goose* at the fuel dock for his return run to San Miguel, he saw Paul Bevlen's tiny helicopter take off from the flat roof of the *News-Star* building and wing across the harbor with rotors flapping, heading westward up the channel.

An hour later, when Tommy's speedboat was still less than halfway to the island, Bevlen buzzed him on the return flight, giving Tommy the okay sign to indicate that he had delivered the photographs to the boss on San Miguel.

When he was still fifteen miles short of his destination, Tommy was alarmed to hear the deep, rhythmic roar of the *Galloping Goose*'s engine cough, sputter and die. Since he was no expert on marine engines—Tommy's only mechanical experience was with sports cars—the power failure gave him real cause for concern.

In case of a real emergency, of course, he had but to radio the Coast Guard for a tow; but his main concern was to rejoin his friends on San Miguel as soon as possible.

During the two hours it took Tommy to track down the difficulty—seawater in the fuel line—a head wind had drifted him back another five miles.

Thus it was nearing sundown when the *Galloping Goose* headed through the precarious slot of Devil's Jaw, instead of the midafternoon deadline Tommy had set for his arrival.

No one answered the blast of his air horn as he threaded through the kelp of Cuyler Harbor and swung around astern of the *Triton IV*, preparatory to tying up on the lee side of the barge.

"Everybody must be up on the hill gravedigging," Tommy muttered, cutting off the engine and snatching up a gaff hook to bring the launch alongside the rubber-tire bumpers that lined the hull of the barge.

Tommy was surprised to see that Ed Morin had brought the RUM tractor back on shore. It was sitting on the beach at the spot where it had originally entered the water, the electromechanical arm and claw retracted, the cable fully wound on its drum except for the two hundred feet or so leading to the controls in the hut.

After he had tied up the speedboat Tommy had a look at the radar shack through binoculars. It was empty, but through the half-open door Tommy could see the sunlight refracting from the safety glass covers of the TV screens.

The fact that the RUM was returned from the deep meant that Gerlock had concluded his photography of the movie prop galleon and no longer needed the RUM's television floodlights.

Scanning the sand-drifted wall of the island above the harbor, Tommy tried to find tracks indicating that the shore party had spent the afternoon tracing the zigzag lines of the Cabrillo chart, using the photo prints Bevlen had delivered by helicopter earlier in the day.

But nothing moved on the desolate, treeless slopes of San Miguel Island. For the first time a tremor of anxiety prickled the hairs on the nape of Tommy's neck. Instinct warned him that something was wrong.

Tommy started climbing the rope ladder to board the *Triton IV*. He had hardly left the cabin roof level of the *Galloping Goose* when a harsh voice thundered from overhead:

"Just hold it where you are, Tommy, or I'll shoot to kill!"

Startled out of his wits, Tommy looked up, his first thought being that someone was trying to joke with him.

Then he saw Dr. Bonilla peering down at him, his face taut and hostile. In his right hand was the stubby barrel of a .38 revolver. The hammer was at full cock, and the muzzle was pointed straight at Tommy's head.

In that instant, Tommy knew his premonition was all too true.

"Where's the sheriff, Tommy?" snarled Bonilla. He looked different, somehow, and it took Tommy a moment to see why: he was no longer wearing the phoney eye-patch disguise over his left eyesocket.

"The sheriff?" echoed Tommy.

"Yes, the sheriff. That's who you went back to town to pick up today, wasn't it? That and because Kleveland wanted his four-eyed brat safe at home before the showdown came, over here on the island."

Tommy swallowed hard. He was suspended on the rope ladder a dozen feet above the cockpit of the *Galloping Goose* and still several rungs short of the level of the barge's deck. If Bonilla jerked trigger at this point-blank range he couldn't possibly miss. What calamity had occurred during his absence today?

"The sheriff," Tommy said, controlling his panic with an effort, "is in Los Angeles—or at Disneyland, to be exact. What's the gun for, sir?"

Knots of muscle swelled in the corners of Bonilla's cheeks. His narrow-set eyes reminded Tommy of a rattlesnake's.

"One more question before I let you ask any," rasped Bonilla. "Did you bring the one hundred thousand dollar draft from the bank? Kleveland's helicopter pilot who delivered the pictures of that silly lead plate said he didn't know anything about a bank draft."

Tommy tried desperately to think of the right thing to say. On his answer might depend whether he would be alive twenty seconds from now.

"Let me—come aboard," he panted. "I'll—explain everything."

For a moment Tommy thought Bonilla was going to shoot him in cold blood. He could see the knuckle of the outlaw's trigger finger whiten under increased pressure.

Then, as if coming to a decision, Bonilla tipped his pistol skyward and backed off a step, beckoning Tommy to come on up the ladder.

Gaining the deck of the barge, Tommy had a frantic glance around, steeling himself for the grisly ordeal of seeing corpses littered here and there. He saw no one, dead or alive.

"Okay, now," Bonilla said, once more lifting his .38 revolver to give Tommy an end-on view of its black and menacing bore. "You were going to explain about that one hundred thousand dollar check?"

Tommy licked his lips. "The—the bank wouldn't—issue such a large—check to a teenager," he husked out. "Not even Spud, without a written order from Mr. Kleveland."

The explanation sounded plausible. Apparently it convinced Bonilla, for he said, "I knew as much. I was a fool for not holding the kid as hostage and sending Kleveland to town to pick up the money himself."

Screwing up his courage, Tommy asked the question that had been preying on his mind ever since he had switched off the engine of the *Galloping Goose* and heard no sign of life: "Wh-where is everyone, Dr. Bonilla?"

At that moment Kurt Gerlock, dressed in swimming trunks and cleated sandals, emerged from the messroom doorway. He was carrying a short length of insulated wire.

"Turn your back to me, Tommy!" snapped Gerlock. "Lou, why you don't chuck these characters over the side for the sharks I'll never know."

Tommy obeyed orders. He felt Gerlock jerk his arms behind his back and knot his wrists together, so tightly that the wire restricted the circulation in his hands.

"Kurt, if I thought you had intelligence enough to understand I would draw you a picture of why I'm not chucking these characters into the bay at this time," Bonilla snapped. "It so happens that we're taking a little trip to Santa Bonita with Kleveland—and the only thing that will make him sign his name to a one hundred thousand dollar cash withdrawal is the knowledge that there are hostages at San Miguel whose lives depend on his cooperation. And the more hostages, the better off we are."

Tommy drew hope from Bonilla's outburst; he seemed to have intimated that the others—Ed Morin, Captain Tucker, and Chester Kleveland—were still alive.

"All right, move along to the galley pantry," Gerlock snapped. "That's where you'll be spending what's left of your life, in case you're interested."

Tommy stumbled over the coaming leading into the messroom and headed toward the door of the galley pantry, which had been slid shut and was latched on the outside with a steel bar fitting into brackets.

Bonilla remained on deck. Tommy's last glimpse of him through a porthole showed the fake Spaniard pocketing his pistol and preparing to go down the ladder to inspect the launch.

Reaching the pantry door, Gerlock lifted the bar in its socket and slid the steel panel to one side. Seated on the deck there, trussed hand and foot, were the three missing adventurers.

"Get in and squat down," Gerlock ordered, "so I can tie your feet. And no false moves, no funny notions, Tommy—or you'll get my diver's knife in your ribs. I don't go along with Lou Weber on this hostage business. I'm for taking my fifty thousand dollars and scramming out while the scramming's good, but Weber, he's greedy. Always greedy.''

Tommy seated himself on the galley floor facing the others and put his legs together as Gerlock ordered. Producing another scrap of wire from somewhere, Gerlock proceeded to truss Tommy's legs cruelly at knees and ankles.

That done, Gerlock stepped back into the messroom, trundled the steel door shut, and dropped the steel bar.

For a long moment no one said anything. Tommy saw an ugly purple-green bruise on Mr. Kleveland's left cheek, where he probably had been struck with a gun barrel. There was a crust of blood on a gash on Ed Morin's forehead. Captain Tucker appeared uninjured but in extreme discomfort from the tightness of his bonds.

Finally Tommy said, ''What happened?''

Mr. Kleveland shrugged. ''Bonilla—real name Lou Weber—got panicky when he saw Paul's helicopter coming. He was afraid it was the law. After Paul delivered the pictures of the Cabrillo chart and took off, Bonilla waited until Ed had brought the RUM tractor back on shore—''

Morin cut in bleakly, ''Only because I had Gerlock swimming along behind the tractor to keep the coaxial cable from snagging on rocks and kelp as the drum rewound it.''

''Anyway,'' Kleveland went on in a despondent voice, ''no sooner had Ed brought the RUM tractor up on the beach, and Gerlock had shed his spear gun and scuba tanks over in the radar shack, than Bonilla put on his Dr. Jekyll-Mr. Hyde act. He whipped off his phoney eye patch and took out a gun and said, 'This farce has gone on long enough. As soon as Tommy Rockford gets back with the launch, we're getting out of here.'''

Thus had begun a reign of terror for the three men left on San Miguel Island. At gun's point, Ed and Kleveland had been forced to board the skiff and row the two crooks back to the *Triton IV*. Captain Tucker, busy preparing their supper in the galley, was unaware of trouble afoot until Gerlock and Bonilla herded their two prisoners into the messroom.

Tucker glanced around the tiny pantry with a wry grin. ''They tied us up like chickens in a butcher shop, removed all the knives and anything else we might use for weapons, and locked us up—with an

144

ultimatum. That was less than an hour before you showed up, Tommy.''

"There wasn't any way we could warn you not to enter the harbor," Ed Morin said apologetically.

Tommy said, "What was the ultimatum?"

The others looked at Chester Kleveland. The newspaperman said, "I had to promise to go to Santa Bonita with them in the launch, acting as if nothing was wrong, and cash them a one hundred and fifty thousand dollar ransom at the bank in return for sparing your lives."

"And you accepted?" Tommy said.

"I refused," Kleveland said, without a trace of heroics in his voice, "because even if I paid them a million dollars, they would double-cross us. That's when Gerlock clouted me on the cheekbone with his gun barrel."

Tommy felt his heart swell with admiration for Kleveland. In the past he had rather regarded Spud's father as an arrogant millionaire stuffed shirt, but he realized now why Kleveland had won two medals for valor in World War II. He had guts.

"I'm hoping," Kleveland went on, "that they'll realize I mean business and take the launch and go. They've got my fifty thousand dollars—nice wages for the few weeks they spent cooking up this swindle. Even if they leave us tied here in the galley, we'd be rescued by the Navy. They wouldn't start bombing practice as long as a big craft like this barge was still anchored in the harbor."

Tommy commented, "I heard Bonilla—Lou Weber—telling Gerlock he was taking you to the bank, Mr. Kleveland. They are expecting you to weaken, I guess."

Suddenly footsteps sounded in the galley outside, the steel bar rasped out of its sockets and the sliding door opened.

Lou Weber stood there, wearing a bulky life jacket. His fist still clutched the stubby-barreled pistol with which he had captured Tommy. Gerlock, the subordinate rather than the leader now that the true character of the partners was exposed, hovered in the background. He was also wearing a life jacket.

"We're ready to leave for Santa Bonita, Kleveland," the erstwhile "Dr. Bonilla" announced. "My friend Gerlock thinks he can operate the launch and he will serve as pilot, since you refuse to do so. The truth of the matter is that Gerlock does not trust me. He thinks I will get the ransom and pull out, leaving him to hold the bag here."

Kleveland said wearily, "I have told you, I will not do business with either of you. Even if I paid over the ransom I would have no guarantee that my friends would be spared."

Ed Morin spoke up quickly: "A launch the size of the *Goose* couldn't make it safely anyway, the way the wind is rising. You'd swamp trying to get through the Devil's Jaw."

As if to emphasize Morin's warning, a huge groundswell lifted and dropped the Triton IV, snapping its anchor chains taut, with a jerk that staggered both of the outlaws.

"Very well, we will postpone our departure until tomorrow," Lou Weber said, "but if you still refuse to cooperate, Kleveland, you will see your friends shot to death before your very eyes. I think you will change your mind about being a hero."

With which ultimatum Weber shut and barred the sliding door.

CHAPTER TWENTY

PROWLER AT MIDNIGHT

T ommy Rockford broke the silence that followed the closing of their prison door by saying, "Engine trouble delayed me this afternoon, but I can see now it was a blessing in disguise. I'm expecting the sheriff to show up by daylight in his helicopter. That should interrupt Weber's plans."

Captain Tucker smiled thinly. "It could also mean the sheriff's doom, Tommy. It seems that Gerlock hadn't thrown away the bolt of my .45-70 rifle after all. He was testing out the sights this afternoon—and bagged a sea gull on the wing. That's real sharp-shooting, with a rifle. Bagging a helicopter at two thousand feet would be simple."

A gloomy silence bore down on the helpless four. Finally Tommy again sought relief in talking.

"While I was in town," he said, "I found out from the *News-Star* files that our phantom galleon was a movie prop Gerlock had burned and sunk back in 1953. That must have been the start of his scheme to swindle you with the Cabrillo business, Mr. Kleveland."

The newspaper publisher nodded. "They told us all about how ingenious they were, including the Spanish galleon business. Well, I swallowed the bait, hook, line, sinker and rowboat. On the TV screen it certainly looked like an authentic galleon to me."

Tommy said, "I'd like to hear what they told you about scheming up this mess, if you don't mind talking."

Kleveland laughed bitterly. "If I don't talk, I'll go crazy," he admitted. "It's up to me whether to play ball with those crooks, or defy them. Either way, I know they'll double-cross us.''

Kleveland's story, summarizing what the two conspirators had bragged about within their prisoners' hearing, so absorbed Tommy's attention that for a while he forgot their desperate peril.

Lou Weber had previously impersonated Dr. Antonio Bonilla of Seville, in a hoax involving a sale of counterfeit Spanish armor to a wealthy Englishman, before he met Kurt Gerlock in London. The latter had just completed the filming of a motion picture when the two met in an antique dealer's shop.

"Weber was admiring an oil painting of a Manila galleon when Gerlock happened to mention that he was in pictures and had sunk a full-scale replica of such a galleon off the California coast," Kleveland recounted. "When Gerlock mentioned that it was still lying in six fathoms off San Miguel Island, Weber brought up the name of Cabrillo, the discoverer of California who was supposed to be buried on San Miguel.

"One thing must have led to another between them," Kleveland went on. "Mention of Cabrillo brought up the matter of the five hundred thousand dollar bounty the Spanish government was offering for the return of the explorer's bones—the authentication of which depended upon the professional opinion of Dr. Bonilla of the Musuem of the Indies, the fine arts expert whom Lou Weber had already impersonated, because of his physical resemblance to the real Dr. Bonilla.

"So they joined forces, and the rest of the plot practically wrote itself. Weber is an expert on Spanish history and archaic language, so he drew up the fake logbook of the *St. Regis* for Gerlock to photograph, and he also carved the San Miguel map on a chunk of lead for Gerlock to plant on the movie prop galleon. He did that only six weeks before he let me in on his big logbook secret—and like an idiot, I fell for his story.''

Tommy said, "Spud told me Sunday that Mr. Kleveland had sent a cablegram to Dr. Bonilla in Seville, and received an answer from Spain. How did they work that?''

Mr. Kleveland laughed sardonically. "They had anticipated that. Antonio Bonilla is a common name in Spain—like John Smith here in America, I guess. Anyway, Weber had a confederate in Seville, ready to accept any mail or cables sent in the name of Antonio Bonilla. If I hadn't been such an utter fool I would have ignored the mailing address Gerlock gave me and sent my cable directly to the Museum of the Indies."

Ed Morin said gently, "Don't feel so bad about it, Mr. Kleveland. That pair did an expert job of baiting the trap. Anybody would have fallen for it."

Tommy mused, "I wonder how far they carried the scheme? I mean, did they visit San Miguel and actually bury a human skeleton at the spot indicated by the Maltese cross on the chart, do you suppose?"

To Tommy's surprise, Kleveland nodded in the affirmative.

"If it hadn't been for your DX radio contact turning up the real Dr. Bonilla and throwing a monkey wrench into their whole scheme," the publisher said to K6ATX, "the map would have led us up to the plateau and we would have exhumed a genuine human skeleton—which Gerlock purchased from a museum, claiming he wanted it for a motion picture—and the bones would have been found encased in a suit of genuine Sixteenth Century Portuguese armor, which Weber contributed."

"In fact," put in Captain Tucker, "they counterfeited the whole business so expertly that I imagine the real Dr. Bonilla might have been fooled into okaying the five hundred thousand dollar reward. As it is, the bones belonged to some California Indian, and the secret of Cabrillo's lost grave is as·far from solution as it ever was."

Darkness blanked out the porthole that was the pantry's only source of illumination. All they could do was make themselves as comfortable as possible in their cramped positions. The restricted confines of the room made it impossible to stretch out on the deck.

They heard Gerlock and Bonilla rattling dishes out in the galley as they prepared their supper, and later they heard a radio blaring music. Finally, around ten o'clock, the two conspirators apparently retired to their bunks, for no further sounds came from them.

Captain Tucker, the oldest man in the party, was apparently resigned to his fate, for he was soon snoring peacefully. Ed Morin and Mr. Kleveland drifted off to sleep because they suffered from nervous exhaustion. But to Tommy, the youngest and presumably the strongest in the group, sleep refused to come.

The air was beginning to get foul in the pantry compartment, the porthole ventilator being hermetically sealed by its rubber gaskets—which meant that death by asphyxiation was possible if Gerlock and Weber decided to abandon them here.

Sheriff Ross Jackson would head for San Miguel by helicopter as soon as he had contacted his office long enough to read the report Tommy had left for him; but he was not due to return from Los Angeles until probably one o'clock tomorrow morning. Five o'clock was the earliest the sheriff could reasonably be expected to reach San Miguel. By then their air supply might have been exhausted.

Crouched there in the blackness, listening to the disturbed breathing of his fellow prisoners, Tommy tried desperately to find respite in sleep. The night was filled with sound: the creaking of timbers and clank of metal as the *Triton IV* rose and fell to the lift of the groundswells crashing into the harbor, the muffled strokes of the ship's bell in the wheelhouse chiming the half hours of the night watch.

At eight bells, indicating midnight, Tommy was beginning to feel drowsy, when an alien sound snapped him fully alert. Someone was removing the steel bar from the door latch. He distinctly heard the metal rubbing metal, and then the faint rumble of ball-bearing runners on the sliding door track.

A nameless fear put its acid taste on Tommy's tongue as he watched the door open, and felt a welcome inrush of pure air from the galley and messroom beyond.

The obvious explanation was that either Gerlock or Weber was standing watch and was making a midnight check on their prisoners. If so, why was he taking so much pains to open the pantry door stealthily and with a minimum of noise? Surely their captors were not so solicitous about not disturbing them.

Tommy, because he was the last prisoner admitted to the cubicle, was closest to the doorway. By the faint glare of starlight coming through the galley's skylight, Tommy could discern the silhouetted figure of whoever had opened the door. It was too small to be Gerlock, too skinny to be Lou Weber.

"Tommy! Dad!"

The figure called out in a barely detectable whisper, but the voice was familiar to Tommy.

"Spud! Is that you?"

The figure came closer, reached out a hand, touched Tommy on the knee and recoiled.

"Yes!" came the unmistakeable voice of Spud Kleveland. "Are you all right? Where are the others?"

Tommy's head was spinning with confusion. Was he dreaming

this? He had left Spud Kleveland in Santa Bonita fifty miles away. Then what was the kid doing aboard *Triton IV*, prowling the deckhouse at midnight?

"We're all in here—wired hand and foot," Tommy whispered back. "Spud—how on earth did you get here? Are you alone? Did Ross Jackson fly you over tonight?"

The pink glow of Spud's fingers clasped over the lens of a flashlight admitted a quick glow of illumination into the pantry, enough to show Spud the sleeping figures of his father, Ed Morin and the captain.

"I'm alone," Spud whispered, switching off the flashlight. "You brought me back yourself, Tommy. I stowed away on the *Galloping Goose* after you and I said good-by at the plaza."

Now Tommy was sure this was a crazy nightmare, not reality.

"You stowed away on the launch? That's impossible!"

Spud was beginning to untwist the wire that bound Tommy's knees and ankles.

"I'm here, ain't I?" retorted Spud, who was seldom ungrammatical. "I crawled into one of the lifejacket cabinets in the cockpit—the ones with the cushioned benches for lids. It was a real cozy trip, out of the spray and wind."

Tommy whispered, "If you'd so much as sneezed I would have turned around and brought you back."

"I know. Dad will be furious with me. But I couldn't bear to miss out on the climax of my first big newspaper story, Tommy...Now turn around and let me work on your arms."

Tommy's legs were so numb he was not even aware that Spud had freed them. Spud set to work on the wires that held his wrists together behind his back, and the circulation had been cut off for so long that he was barely aware when his arms came free.

One by one Spud awakened the others, saving his father for the last. Even though they owed their lives to Spud, the boy knew his presence at the island represented insubordination. As it was, his father almost shouted his son's name, so great was his surprise.

"If I hadn't been peeking through the lid of the lifejacket box where I stowed away, so that I saw Dr. Bonilla threaten to shoot Tommy on his way on board the barge, I would have been captured too," Spud said with a shudder. "When Dr. Bonilla came down to the launch I died a thousand deaths for fear he would find me. He would have, if he had opened the box on my side of the cockpit."

It was all the four prisoners could do to regain their feet after Spud had finished his rescue work.

"I came aboard at eleven o'clock," Spud explained, "and I snooped all over the barge except where Gerlock and Bonilla are sleeping. I almost didn't look in this pantry. I—I was afraid you'd all been—killed and—tossed to the sharks."

Clinging to each other for support, the four rescued prisoners groped their way out into the galley. Busily massaging their wrists to restore circulation to their benumbed hands, the five held a council of war.

"It would be suicide to try to barge into Stateroom A and over-power those two crooks in their sleep," Captain Tucker said.

"We could go up to the wheelhouse and put a Mayday distress call on the radio," suggested Ed Morin.

"Too risky," vetoed Mr. Kleveland. "If we make the slightest noise and wake up that pair, they'll shoot us like rats. I think our best bet is to board the launch and head outside the bar. That would leave Bonilla—Weber—and Kurt Gerlock marooned. We could stand by until the sheriff shows up in the morning and let him take over from there. How does that sound?"

Everyone was agreed that discretion was the better part of valor, considering the fact that the enemy was armed and desperate, and they had no weapons.

"Let's go," whispered Tommy. "We'll pole the launch around under the stern counter out of sight before we start the engine. By the time Gerlock and Weber wake up and come to investigate, we should be through the Devil's Jaw and out of gunshot range."

The five of them headed in single file out the galley door and along the narrow walkway of the portside deck. Tommy and Spud were wearing rubber-soled sneakers which made no noise, but the three men had to remove their shoes and creep along in their socks.

Enough starlight leaked through holes in the overcast for them to find the rope ladder leading down to the *Galloping Goose*. When they were all aboard the launch, Ed Morin took command as befitted the owner of the craft. "Tommy, stand by to cast off the bow line. Captain Tucker, you handle my stern line and I'll use the gaff hook to pole us along to the stern of the barge. Spud, you and your father get inside the cabin and stay out of the way."

Before the various fugitives had a chance to get to their assigned spots they heard voices on the barge overhead, followed by a clatter of feet running along the deck.

Had they been discovered?

One of the *Triton IV*'s big five thousand candle power searchlights snapped on from the deckhouse roof, sending a pencil of white light across the cove to lay a silver disk against the sandy hillside above the radar hut. Then came an angry shout from above: "The launch! They're on the launch!"

The voice was Lou Weber's, and it was followed by the ear-riving crash of a rifle shot. Tommy saw the powder flash spew from the Winchester muzzle. It was angled down at the launch, the .45-70 bullet smashing through the fiberglass roof of the cabin as if it had been tissue paper and drilling the sonar gear inside with a chiming tinkle of fractured glass.

Atop the deckhouse, Gerlock was swiveling the big searchlight beam around preparatory to angling the spotlight down on the *Galloping Goose* to illuminate targets for Weber's stolen rifle.

"Dive for it!" yelled Tommy Rockford. "It's our only chance!"

"And swim for the beach!" Ed Morin's shout reached Tommy's ears a split second before his diving body cleft the waters of the harbor with a geysering splash.

Two fathoms under, Tommy saw the black water turn green and saw his own shadow on the sandy bottom, which meant Gerlock had trained the searchlight on the launch. He heard the pluck of bullets ricocheting off the water, and *kerplunk*ing noises which could only be his companions making belated dives.

Swimming underwater until his lungs were almost bursting, Tommy touched bottom and stood up in water barely armpit deep.

The searchlight was playing over the cove, pausing whenever Gerlock spotted a swimmer surfacing for air. Instantly the night seemed to explode to the concussion of Weber's rifle shots, but from the way the two criminals were cursing, Tommy got the impression that all five of them had made a clean getaway.

Ducking under, Tommy swam the remaining distance to shore and crawled out of the water, only to flatten himself instantly in the shelter of a driftlog as Gerlock's searchlight beam hunting rifle targets raced along the beach and passed over him.

Another figure crawled ashore a few yards away—Ed Morin,

draped with ribbon kelp. Captain Tucker was swimming ashore in Ed's wake.

Then Gerlock's spotlight focused on Spud and his father as the two Klevelands scrambled ashore fifty yards farther west. They turned east, instinctively heading for the shelter of the concrete radar hut, when Weber opened fire as rapidly as he could lever cartridges into the breech of the .45-70.

Slugs kicked up little spurts of sand inches from the feet of the sprinting father and son, and then the gunfire cut off, as suddenly as it had started, despite the fact that the targets were in easy range and Gerlock was holding them in the traveling beam of the searchlight.

"Magazine's empty," Tommy called to Morin, who was helping the badly-winded Tucker wade ashore. "Let's get to the radar shack before he can reload."

Gerlock switched off the searchlight, leaving the Klevelands to stagger their way along the beach to join the other three.

"You guys ain't goin' anywhere!" came Gerlock's hate-filled taunt. "Come daylight, Lou an' me will come ashore and track you down easy enough, the whole lot of you. It'll be like shootin' fish in a rain barrel."

Assembling at the inshore side of the radar hut, the five fugitives held a council of war.

Chester Kleveland suggested forting up in the radar hut until the sheriff's arrival with the helicopter, but Ed Morin vetoed the suggestion vigorously.

"They'd have us trapped, sir. They could fire on us through the observation slot, or dump gasoline from the generator tank onto us and cremate us alive."

Captain Tucker said grimly, "But there's no place to hide on the island. I've explored it from one end to the other. A tumbledown sheep barn up on the plateau, and what brush there is in the gully that leads to the top. Unless we could hide in the sea lion caves over on Bennett's Point at the west end of the island—and I'd rather take my chance with Weber and Gerlock than I would those bull sea lions."

Tommy Rockford said, "We've got only four hours left before daylight. Let's head up the gully and see if we can hide near the Navy's airstrip. That's where Ross Jackson would be landing his chopper.

CHAPTER TWENTY-ONE

HELICOPTER PASSENGER

T
he first gray streaks of dawn found Tommy Rockford lying
on his stomach at the brink of San Miguel's upper plateau,
taking advantage of the slim concealment of a rock cairn and
small marble cross marking the "Cabrillo Monument" which a
Portuguese-American society had placed there in 1937 in honor of the
discoverer of California.

At his back was the mile-long blacktop paving of the Navy's
airstrip, now streaked with long sand dunes which the northwest winds
kept continually shifting. On the south side of the landing field, a couple of hundred feet from where Tommy had posted himself for lookout
duty, stood the ramshackle remains of a sheep-shearing shed dating
from the period when San Miguel had been a sheep ranch.

Inside that flimsy shelter, Tommy's four companions were taking a much-needed sleep. They realized the weatherbeaten structure,
with its south wall entirely gone, would offer no protection from the
bullets of Kurt Gerlock and Lou Weber; but there were enough other
ruined ranch buildings in the vicinity to provide shelter for a time-
stalling game of hide and seek, once the two outlaws made their
appearance.

Six hundred feet below Tommy's vantage point was the kelp-
mottled crescent of Cuyler Harbor, with the unlovely rectangular bulk
of the *Triton IV* imprisoned there by her four anchors. The radar shack
stood out prominently because of the big target plus sign which the
pilots of Navy missile planes would zero in on when bombing prac-

tice was resumed.

Twenty minutes after sunrise, Tommy saw Gerlock and Weber emerge from the deckhouse of the Barge, the latter toting Captain Tucker's long-range hunting rifle.

Instead of boarding the *Galloping Goose*, which neither had the know-how to operate, the two conspirators climbed into the *Triton IV*'s rowboat and headed for the beach, Gerlock handling the oars with practiced skill.

Both men were laughing and joking, their banter reaching Tommy's ear on the edge of the plateau six hundred feet up the sandy slope.

Unaware that Ross Jackson was expected on the island today, believing they had all day at their disposal before the Navy sent its scouting plane over the harbor at dusk, Gerlock and Bonilla seemed to be looking forward to their manhunt with keen relish.

They had reason to feel smug and complacent. They had heard enough about the island—and Gerlock had visited San Miguel himself not too many weeks ago, burying the fake Cabrillo skeleton somewhere up here—to know that there was no place where one fugitive, let alone five, could hide.

After hauling the dory up above high-tide mark, the two outlaws made a perfunctory visit to the radar hut, satisfied themselves that it was empty, and then strolled along the beach to make sure no one was hiding behind the RUM tractor.

The only possible way up the steep hillside overlooking the entire perimeter of the harbor was a brushy gulch, or barranca, which the Geodetic Survey chart showed as the location of the old trail up to the sheep ranch back in the 1930's.

Toward the gully the two man-hunters now made their way. Once inside it, even a blind man could read trail sign. The five who had escaped from the *Triton IV* the previous night had left their footprints on the brushy, weed-grown trail, which had been sheltered from the night winds that swept in from the sea.

The old trail was steep, with many switchbacks, and last night it had taken Tommy and his friends the better part of an hour to climb to the level mesa at the top. Even by daylight, Tommy knew Gerlock and Weber would not reach the plateau and start their manhunt much before forty minutes had elapsed.

Starting the elapsed-time function on his solar-powered

wristwatch, Tommy squirmed back away from the Cabrillo Monument and, coming to his feet, set off across the landing field in a southwesterly direction.

Here at break of day the wind had died down, so that Tommy left a distinct set of tracks in the rippled blowsand which covered the landing strip to a depth of several inches. That trail would be the first thing the two manhunters would see—and if Tommy's plan worked it would decoy them away from the old sheep barns, lying to the southeast.

Once in the rock and brush country beyond the airstrip, Tommy left the sand dunes and legged it at top speed for the sheep ranch buildings. The wind of the night before had long since blotted out the tracks they had made in heading for the buildings silhoutted against the stars last night.

Threading in and out of the jumbled piles of boards and rusting machinery which marked the former ranch buildings, Tommy dogtrotted into the sheep barn to find all four of his companions sleeping the drugged sleep of exhaustion.

He decided to wait another twenty minutes before awakening them. That would give them time for a conference before Gerlock and Weber topped the rim of the plateau and began their stalking game.

At least two of their number were relatively safe from being shot on sight—Ed Morin, whom they needed to pilot the get-away launch, and Chester Kleveland, who, the conspirators believed, could be made to pay a ransom running into six figures, if they played their cards correctly.

Tommy and Spud were the two most vulnerable to being shot without mercy if Weber succeeded in spotting them in the telescopic sight of Tucker's rifle. Tommy was the radio ham responsible for breaking up their well-laid plans, and in Spud the two criminals would be sure to recognize the fifth person who had released their prisoners from the galley pantry at midnight. How Spud had reached San Miguel was a mystery they would solve later.

Stationing himself at a window of the sheep shed, Tommy kept his eyes on the patch of greasewood and sagebrush marking the mouth of the gulch which led to the harbor. It was there Gerlock and Bonilla would be reappearing.

It was extremely doubtful if Sheriff Jackson would arrive before noon at the earliest, for the entire twenty-five-mile expanse of water between the Islands and Point Concepcion was socked in solid with fog, making a helicopter flight impossible.

Southward, toward the open Pacific, the sky was blue.

Waiting for the two manhunters to appear became an intolerable strain. Taking flight and heading for the ocean was not worth considering—not with sharks reported off San Miguel all summer.

Tommy envied the others, sleeping like dead men a few feet away.

Suddenly a shift in the breeze brought to the boy's ears the throb of an aircraft motor. It was not a multi-engine craft, and it didn't sound like a small private plane, either.

The wind shifted before Tommy could orient the sound, but he believed it came from the southeast, toward the woolly cloud bank that overhung Santa Rosa Island.

"It sounded like a helicopter engine, by gosh!"

Very possibly Ross Jackson was cruising above the fog ceiling which, Tommy knew from experience, would be dissipated by the burning July sun before the morning was half spent.

Suddenly, like some great wing-flapping bird, a helicopter materialized out of the cloud over Santa Rosa Island. It was little over a mile away and was obviously starting a circle of San Miguel Island as if to reconnoiter.

"Wake up—wake up!" Tommy shouted, running into the sheep shed to rouse his exhausted friends. "I'm not sure, but I think Ross Jackson's chopper is coming in."

As soon as the others were on their feet, watching the ungainly-looking whirlybird descending toward the flat top of San Miguel, Tommy gave them the real eye-opener:

"Gerlock and Weber are coming up the same trail we took last night." He glanced at the elapsed-time dial on his watch. "They've been on the trail exactly twenty-three minutes, so they are probably halfway up the hillside."

Tommy ran out into the open, snatching up an old scrap of burlap and waving it to attract the attention of the pilot of the oncoming helicopter.

It was the sheriff, all right; Tommy recognized the big six-pointed gold star, symbol of the Santa Barbara County Sheriff's Aerial Squadron, glistening on the fuselage.

"This is working out too well to be true," Tommy told himself, hoping the two crooks hadn't spotted the helicopter, and doubting that they could hear it from down below the brow of that hill.

In response to Tommy's frantic wavings, Ross Jackson set the chopper down on its ski-type landing gear on the south side of the sheep barn, instead of on the asphalt-paved landing strip on the north side, which had been his original intention.

Waving Tommy back until the rotors had stopped turning, the sheriff turned to a passenger sharing the plexiglass-bubble cabin with him, and then unlatched the exit door.

"Those two crooks are chasing us and they're armed, Ross!" Tommy blurted the bad news to the lawman before Jackson had a chance to step to the ground. "They're coming up the barranca from the harbor and they'll be showing up inside of twenty minutes, I would say—"

Ross Jackson reached up to pat the gray, no-nonsense stock of the automatic rifle slung over his right shoulder.

"I've got a hot welcome waiting for Lou Weber," the sheriff said. "Thanks to those fingerprints you got for me, Tommy, and some quick work by the FBI boys, I've got enough on Lou Weber to send him to the slammer forever. But Scotland Yard has first claim on him— for murder back on 1978."

Then, for the first time, Tommy Rockford caught sight of the man who had flown out to San Miguel aboard Jackson's chopper.

"Tony—EA7WK!" Tommy exclaimed, recognizing the bald head, the flesh-colored eye patch, and the Spanish cavalier mustache and goatee. "Gosh, I'm glad to meet you—I'm K 6 Alfa Tango X-ray!"

The real Antonio Bonilla, distinguished curator of the Museum of the Indies in Seville, reached out to shake the hand of the radio ham whose DX QSO from Washington State last Saturday night had brought him winging six thousand miles by jet to reach this desolate isle where Cabrillo had perished so long ago.

"Since I am indirectly responsible for the difficulties you wrote about in the report our friend Ross Jackson read me in Santa Bonita last night," Dr. Bonilla said in the same rich, accented voice which Tommy recalled from his single sideband QSO, "I insisted on coming along to be in at the showdown. I have looked forward to meeting this Lou Weber for many years, Tomás—but not with the pleasure I looked forward to in meeting K6ATX."

There was no time for introducing Dr. Bonilla to the others.

Tommy explained, "Since it's behind the barn, they won't see the helicopter until it's too late. And the minute they show their faces above the plateau rim, I'll let 'em get a glimpse of me to decoy them over here, in range of that M-16."

The sheriff motioned for the others to station themselves out of sight, including Dr. Bonilla. Reaching back into the cabin of his chopper, the sheriff took out a battery-powered electric megaphone for later use.

Then he and Tommy made their way to the outermost doorway of the sheep barn, facing north toward the harbor.

A sharp cry from Spud, squatting behind a knothole farther along the wall of the abandoned building, was their first inkling that the showdown was at hand.

Several yards to the east of the spot where Tommy had expected to see the two outlaws emerge from the defile, a flash of sunlight on gunmetal drew their eyes to the beefy shape of Lou Weber, climbing up and over the edge of the plateau.

"Make it fast, Tommy!" warned the sheriff, unslinging his automatic rifle. "Don't take any chances."

Tommy emerged from the sheep barn as if intending to head for another ruined building. Then, when he saw Lou Weber lift his .45-70 for a shot, Tommy hit the ground like a runner sliding into second base just as a bullet zinged overhead like a wasp.

Scuttling back inside the barn on all fours, Tommy headed for a handy knothole and put his eye to the aperture just in time to see Kurt Gerlock loom into view. Lou Weber pointed toward the barn, then waved Gerlock to follow him.

"Here come the flies into the spider web!" chuckled Ed Morin, a few feet away behind the rusting remains of a mowing machine.

Although obviously winded from their steep climb up the gully, Weber and Gerlock broke into a trot as they headed across the landing strip toward the rickety sheep shed where they had glimpsed Tommy Rockford.

Fifty yards away, the two halted, looking this way and that, heads cocked to pick up the slightest sound.

"You can't get away, so I advise you to come out with your hands up!" shouted Weber, levering a shell into the breech of his Winchester. "If I have to come in there after you, I'll come shooting."

No one moved inside the sheep shed. No one spoke. All eyes were on Sheriff Ross Jackson, crouched just out of sight beside the barn door.

Then Jackson picked up the bullhorn, turned the volume on full, and spoke into the mouthpiece. "Drop the guns and stand where you are, Lou Weber and Kurt Gerlock. This is the county sheriff speaking. You're both covered with an automatic rifle that could cut you off at the pockets if you start running."

Like Jovian thunder, the electrically amplified sound of the sheriff's voice echoed and re-echoed across the barren sand hills of the desert island.

To avoid any nonsense, Jackson thrust the barrel of the M-16 around the edge of the door and triggered a short burst, the slugs stitching a dotted line along the asphalt runway in front of the two bayed outlaws.

"We've had it, Kurt," choked out Lou Weber, and tossed the .45-70 into the nearest clump of chaparral. "We surrender, sheriff."

CHAPTER TWENTY-TWO

FLYING MISSILE TARGETS

The two outlaws, completely demoralized by the unexpected appearance of the sheriff of Santa Barbara County, offered no resistance as Ross Jackson stalked out of the barn behind his fuming M-16 and handcuffed Weber's right wrist to Gerlock's left.

"Don't give me any hogwash about where is my arrest warrant," Jackson cut off Weber's whining protest about the steel manacles. "The FBI teletyped my office a record a yard long about you. It only took the real Dr. Bonilla you were impersonating about twenty-four hours to get from Europe to Los Angeles, with an overnight stopover at Kennedy International Airport. The same length of time from now, you could be in the custody of Scotland Yard in London to answer for the murder of that old antique dealer near Charing Cross."

Lou Weber's swarthy face went the color of a banana peel. He could not take his eyes off the Spanish archaeologist whose identity he had assumed in the past. This was their first face-to-face meeting.

"It's too bad we don't have time to dig into a shallow grave not fifty feet from this spot, Dr. Bonilla," Weber said. "I'd wager you any sum you name that you would identify the bones and armor you'd find there as being those of Juan Rodriguez Cabrillo."

Before the real Dr. Bonilla could reply, Ross Jackson said brusquely, "We don't have time for playing games. I'll fly Dr. Bonilla back to town in the chopper, because there isn't room for two prisoners. Captain Tucker, with your permission I'd like to see Gerlock and Weber safely locked up aboard your barge. I'll be at the dock to meet you when you land this afternoon, you can be assured of that."

Captain Tucker chuckled. "I know just the brig to clap these hard cases into, sheriff. The pantry off the galley. They won't have a Spud Kleveland to rescue 'em like we did."

Not much more was said until the worn-out party had gone back down the ravine trail, with Ross Jackson and his prisoners leading the way.

Heading toward the rowboat that would take them out to the *Triton IV*, the sheriff caught sight of the RUM tractor parked up the beach toward the east.

"Is that contraption still working?" Jackson asked. "I'd like Dr. Bonilla to see our Yankee ingenuity in action."

Ed Morin said, "If you have time, you can see me run her into the harbor and the crane barge will hoist 'er aboard, Ross."

Jackson said, "How long would that take?"

"Hour, hour and a half. Diving down to set the crane hook for the hoist takes the time."

Jackson glanced at his sullen-faced prisoners.

"I didn't tie down the helicopter," the sheriff said, "and along toward nine-ten o'clock the wind gusts on this island get strong enough to blow a chopper into the wild blue yonder. But I would like Dr. Bonilla to see you wave that mechanical arm around like I've heard you can do at long distance."

Ed Morin headed for the radar shack. "Only take five minutes to demonstrate," he called back. "You folks go inside and shut the door so your eyes will become accustomed to the darkness, and I'll run the RUM into the water and switch on the TV gear."

A few moments later the entire party, including the handcuffed prisoners, were once again back inside the concrete-walled shack. Ed Morin, getting the gasoline engine started on the power generator, joined them a moment later.

Sheriff Jackson, who was an ardent student of electronics as it applied to modern law enforcement, took a position in front of the RUM console where he could also look out the observation slot to see the tractor when Morin started it in motion.

"The first thing we'll do," Ed said, "is have the RUM describe a figure eight on the beach yonder. Then—"

"I beg your pardon," broke in Kurt Gerlock's snarling voice from the rear wall of the shack, "but the first thing we will do is have the sheriff hand over that rifle and the keys to these bracelets."

Of one accord, the others whirled about to face the two outlaws, who the sheriff had ushered into the rear corner of the concrete cubicle.

Weber and Gerlock were still fettered with steel bracelets, wrist to wrist.

But in Gerlock's right hand was a pistol-type grip of his diver's spear gun, the needle-sharp three-pronged harpoon aimed straight at Sheriff Jackson's heart. A whit more pressure on the trigger of that deadly spring-powered underwater gun could drive that barbed spear completely through Jackson's chest.

The stunned tableau remained as motionless as a photograph. In the semidarkness, no one had noticed Gerlock's scuba bottles and his spear gun lying in the corner where he had put them after coming out of the sea yesterday.

Now, between one clock-tick and the next, Gerlock was in full command of the situation, and Ross Jackson knew it.

"Tommy," Jackson said harshly, "the key to those handcuffs is in my right jacket pocket. Get it and do as Gerlock says. I don't want any unnecessary bloodshed around here."

Nausea stabbed Tommy's vitals as he got the handcuff key from the sheriff's pocket.

"Hand me the M-16 first, Tommy," Gerlock ordered. "Hold it by the barrel and hand it to me butt first. No tricks or I'll skewer your sheriff friend like a bug on a pin."

Moving like someone in a nightmare, Tommy took the rifle from the sheriff and handed it butt first to Gerlock, who took the barrel with his handcuffed hand, still holding the speargun on Jackson.

When the handcuff had been unlocked from his wrist, Gerlock set the M-16 carefully on the floor and said to Tommy, "Throw Tucker's Winchester out the door where I can pick it up later."

Tommy did so, the glare of daylight slanting off the placid waters of the cove almost blinding them inside the hut.

"Okay, now hand me the police pistol Jackson carries in his shoulder holster—and the Colt he took off Lou Weber. It's in his pocket."

When Tommy had disarmed the sheriff and dropped the hand guns in the voluminous pockets of Gerlock's parka jacket, the movie diver turned for the first time to Lou Weber, who up to now had been a silent witness of the sudden happy reversal of their fortunes.

"Lou, I never had a criminal record until you came into my life and talked me into this phoney Cabrillo scheme. I'm going to do you a favor, Lou. I'm not going to let Scotland Yard get you."

The man who had impersonated Dr. Bonilla started gibbering with nervous reaction. He saw nothing sinister in Gerlock's words.

"I knew you'd stick by me, Kurt. After all, if it hadn't been for Bonilla being a radio ham, this scheme would have netted us a cool hundred grand. Even so, we've got fifty grand out of it. I—I'll give you half, Kurt."

Gerlock motioned toward the door. "Head for the skiff. I'm taking Morin and the skipper with us, as hostages. The rest stay here."

Lou Weber ducked his head to clear the low lintel of the radar shack door and started down to the water's edge. He was out of range of Tommy's vision when Gerlock stepped to the door, aimed the speargun at his partner's retreating back, and pulled the trigger.

Tommy and the others gasped with horror as they heard the *thwack* of the steel harpoon striking human flesh. They heard no outcry. After what seemed an eternity, they heard the heavy thump of Lou Weber's corpse crashing to the shingle beach.

Gerlock tossed the spear gun aside and picked up the M-16. Backing out of the doorway, he said "Ed and the captain, follow me. You're rowing me over to the barge."

Facing sudden death at the hands of this murderer if they hesitated, Ed and Captain Tucker headed outside, turning their eyes away from the grisly sight of Lou Weber lying on the beach, impaled by a shark harpoon.

"Sheriff," grinned Kurt Gerlock, "I know what you're thinkin'. All you had on me up to now was conspiracy to defraud. Now you've got a murder rap to pin on me. Well"—as he spoke, Gerlock slammed the iron door and snapped the big brass padlock through the hasp— "now you won't be pinning any rap on anybody. Because come this time tomorrow, the Navy missile men will have vaporized this radar hut and everybody in it. I'm going back to Santa Bonita in the *Triton IV*, and when the Navy sees an empty harbor they'll assume the Chester H. Kleveland Expedition has evacuated the island."

Tommy Rockford groped his way to the observation slot and watched in mute horror as Kurt Gerlock herded Ed Morin and Captain Tucker into the rowboat and headed out across the harbor to the anchored barge.

Sheriff Jackson tested the inner knob of the iron door just once, and then gave up any hope of their escaping this reinforced concrete box on their own volition.

"Don't worry about the Navy bombing us," the sheriff said, trying to allay the panic that was building up along with the claustrophobia of this semidark tomb. "As soon as Ed and Tucker get to Santa Bonita they'll telephone the commanding officer at Arguello to rescue us."

Spud Kleveland, as cool as any of them in the face of a terrible death, reached over to pat the sheriff on the arm.

"A nice try, Ross, but it won't go. You know Gerlock will murder Ed and the captain before he goes ashore, and it'll be days before their bodies are found on the barge. By that time Gerlock will have cashed Dad's two checks for fifty thousand dollars and be long gone."

Mr. Kleveland licked his lips. "Perhaps the Navy scout plane will see Weber's body. Or the RUM tractor."

Tommy laughed bleakly. "At ten thousand feet—and the speeds those jets zip over? All they're looking for is a big barge in Cuyler Harbor. No, this is Gerlock's revenge, folks. We might as well resign ourselves to being missile targets."

They watched in sick horror from the observation slot as Ed and the captain climbed the rope ladder with gun-toting Kurt Gerlock bringing up the rear. The three disappeared around the corner of the deckhouse.

Ten minutes later they heard the big diesels come alive inside the *Triton IV*'s hull, followed shortly by the rumble and clank of hoisting winches.

"They're hauling in the anchors," Mr. Kleveland reported. "That means they're fixing to run the Devil's Jaw before the tide is full."

Tommy said glumly, "There'll be water enough in the passage for the barge to make it. If they get stuck, they'll have only a two-hour wait for the tide to float 'em off."

When the fourth and last anchor was hoisted aboard, they saw Captain Tucker's head bobbing behind the windows of the pilot house. The barge was facing south; he would have to turn it around 360° before it was headed for the Devil's Jaw.

Ed Morin, closely followed by Kurt Gerlock, appeared on the forward deck and they stationed themselves near the railing.

"That's for lookout duty, groping through the inlet," Mr. Kleveland said in answer to a low-voiced query from Dr. Bonilla, who up to now had not spoken a syllable.

Morin's binoculars hung from a peg by the RUM console. Using them, Tommy saw that Gerlock had discarded the bulky automatic rifle in favor of a Colt automatic, the muzzle of which was pressing Ed in the ribs.

"They're about to get under way," Chester Kleveland said heavily, "and when that barge leaves the harbor, our last hopes of survival leave with it. Spud, my son, now you can see why I ordered you to stay ashore yesterday."

"Dad," husked out the boy, "I—I'm glad I'm here—with you."

Tommy Rockford spoke into the tension-packed silence that followed: "I don't think we're doomed by a long shot. I think I know a way to beat Gerlock at his own game—and save us all!

CHAPTER TWENTY-THREE

RACE FOR THE DEVIL'S JAW

The others looked at each other as if they feared Tommy's sanity had cracked under the pressure of impending doom.

Almost frantic in his haste, K6ATX elbowed his way through the press of bodies lined up before the observation slot and stationed himself at the console of Ed Morin's RUM tractor.

"If I can only remember how Ed worked these gadgets the other day," panted Tommy, "I can run Ed's tractor into the Devil's Jaw before the barge can get there..."

Tommy's eyes were darting over the bewildering array of meters and rheostats, toggle switches and push buttons, levers and signal lamps which comprised the "brain" to control the RUM which stood parked on the sand dunes two hundred feet away, linked to the control panel by the black rope of coaxial cable.

"What good would that do?" Spud wanted to know. "It won't get us out of this trap—"

Tommy closed a switch marked POWER SUPPLY to send high-voltage electricity surging through the coaxial cable to the motors of the tractor down the beach.

"Tommy's got something!" shouted Sheriff Jackson. "The entrance to this harbor is barely deep enough for navigation as it is. And if Tommy can block that entrance with a three-ton object like the RUM, the *Triton IV* will be sealed up in this cove like a fly in a corked bottle!"

"But," Spud protested, still not understanding the significance of Tommy's idea, "that still won't get us out of—"

"Oh, hush up, Spud!" scolded his father. "What Tommy's trying to do is keep the Navy from using this hut for a missile target. When the patrol plane flies over this evening to make sure we've evacuated San Miguel, and sees that big crane barge still in the harbor, they'll have to send the Coast Guard in to investigate before the missile practice can begin—and we'll be rescued!"

Tommy, concentrating now as he had never concentrated before on a problem, pressed a button labeled MAIN MOTOR: START.

Ammeter needles danced on meter dials, meaning nothing to Tommy's audience, but telling K6ATX that the big motor which propelled the RUM tractor was humming into action, accounting for the extra-heavy drain on the power supply.

"You'd better hurry!" Ross Jackson shouted. "There goes the *Triton IV* toward the Devil's Jaw! They're under way!"

Tommy grated hoarsely, "Captain Tucker's got to turn the barge around first. That'll take time. With the pilothouse up forward, he couldn't back through the Devil's Jaw."

Tommy realized he could not use the RUM's television eye for steering purposes; to switch on the camera in bright sunlight would destroy the ultrasensitive vidicon tube, Ed had said.

"We're ready to roll now," Tommy announced, and jumped over to the observation window to see exactly which way the RUM was headed. The Devil's Jaw, his destination, was due north of the beach. To his dismay, he saw that Ed had left the tractor facing west, after its emergence from the surf yesterday.

Back to the console Tommy jumped. "You guys will have to guide me," he said. "I've got to turn the RUM around ninety degrees before I start it rolling toward the Devil's Jaw." Then, more to himself than to the others, he mumbled his procedures: "Reverse the right-hand track—put the left-hand track into forward—that ought to swing it around to face the harbor..."

Trembling with suspense, Tommy threw the two switches that controlled the tracks, setting them in opposite directions—right reverse, left forward—and then for the first time pushed the main transmission control to put the tractor into operating gear.

"Let me know," Tommy yelled, "when the RUM is headed directly at the Devil's Jaw! I've never piloted this monster before!"

Four pairs of eyes swiveled from the *Triton IV*, which had ponderously completed her full turn so as to head the square prow toward the outlet in the harbor bar, and focused upon the RUM tractor just as Tommy advanced the rheostat marked THROTTLE.

Fascinated by the electronic drama they were witnessing, the spectators saw the RUM's metal cleats begin turning in opposite directions, swiveling the tractor around until it faced due north.

"Stop!" all four yelled in unison. They heard Tommy snapping switches. The RUM became motionless.

Out on the *Triton IV* the men were too busy with their own problems to notice the sudden change of direction of the tractor over on the beach. Ed Morin was at the forward rail, serving as lookout when the barge nosed into the narrow, shallow trough of the Devil's Jaw; immediately at his elbow was Kurt Gerlock, gun winking in the sunlight. Up in the pilothouse, Captain Tucker was having his hands full with steering and engines.

"The barge is starting forward now!" reported Ross Jackson. "She'll probably make about two knots, no more. You're going to have to hurry it if that tractor gets to the Devil's Jaw before the barge does, Tommy!"

Sweat was seeping from Tommy's pores. A quick look at the control panel told him that, so far as he could see, everything was functioning properly.

He snapped both tracks into forward position.

"Here goes!" cried K6ATX. "I'll give her full throttle and hope for the best."

He punched the transmission control button and advanced the throttle rheostat slowly, so as to keep the steel treads of the tractor from digging into the sand.

Ross Jackson and the two Klevelands felt their hearts pick up speed as the RUM lurched forward at Tommy's command and hit the shallow water with a geysering splash which could not fail to attract the attention of the three men on the barge.

"They're trying to ram us with the tractor!" bawled Kurt Gerlock, his stentorian voice carrying distinctly to the occupants of the radar shack. "Full speed ahead, Tucker! We've got to beat that machine through the inlet..."

The RUM was now wallowing half-submerged across the cove, following the harbor bar's sandy, rock-studded ridge. At times, when the tractor hit a low spot on the bar, it sank until only the slowly unwinding cable drum and the mechanical arm and claw were visible

170

above water; then like some shaggy prehistoric monster it climbed back into view, moving inexorably toward the break in the ridge which marked the Devil's Jaw.

"More speed! More speed!" Gerlock was shouting at the top of his lungs, but the *Triton IV* showed no gain in speed.

Tommy had done all he could. He joined the others at the observation slot, and he had Ed Morin's binoculars to follow the outcome of the race between the huge crane barge and the creeping iron turtle with the Cyclopean eye, now on full throttle.

"She's full speed ahead now," shouted Captain Tucker, his head appearing through the window of the wheelhouse. "Keep your shirt on, Kurt—we'll beat that contraption through the gate, don't worry."

To the onlookers in the radar hut it was obvious that Tucker was lying to throw their captor off guard. The RUM was less than fifty yards from the Devil's Jaw now, gaining speed as its spinning treads found more rock and less sand. The *Triton IV* was an equal distance from the channel, but its forward speed was less than half what Tommy was getting out of the RUM.

Suddenly berserk as he saw for himself that the tractor would block the only outlet to the harbor, Gerlock opened fire on the half-submerged mechanical monster with his .45. The slugs ricocheted off the metal cable drum with no more effect than a mosquito stinging a bull elephant.

Tommy swung his glasses toward the prow of the *Triton IV*. He could see Ed Morin swinging into a crouched position, ready to spring on Gerlock the first opportunity that presented itself. Ed had been a judo expert in the Korean war. If Gerlock lowered his guard for as much as a split second he was a dead duck.

"There she goes!" shrieked Chester Kleveland, completely forgetting that he was a dignified middle-aged newspaper editor. "Yippee-ki-yay!! That blocks the channel!"

Keeping his binoculars focused on Gerlock and Ed, through the corner of his eye Tommy saw the RUM hit the brink of the submarine canyon marking the Devil's Jaw channel, teeter there as the grinding treads sought purchase on the rocks, and then lunge forward and somersault out of sight inside the Devil's Jaw—in all probability landing upside down when it reached the bottom of the steep declivity.

Instinctively Tommy turned to the console to shut off the power, but a blaze of red signal lamps told him the RUM had already lost contact with the control panel. In its tumble to the bottom of the Devil's Jaw it had snapped its cable. Blown fuses and tripped relays automatically shut off the power generator outside the hut.

Tommy jumped back to the observation slot and put his binoculars on the *Triton IV*. The prow of the barge was now entering the Devil's Jaw. Up forward, Gerlock was leaning over the rail, peering at the boiling bubbles and churning brown sand marking the spot where the RUM had disappeared.

"Can we clear it?" Gerlock was shouting. "Are we blocked?"

He got his answer in the next instant. The men in the radar shack held their breath as they saw the massive crane barge suddenly stagger, then yaw around as its bow crashed into some sunken menace to navigation. The RUM had won!

The *Triton IV* seemed to hump its back as if in an effort to shove aside the uncharted object into which it had collided—and as that immovable object forced the barge to a dead halt, the sudden jolt and yaw threw Gerlock off balance and for the tenth part of a second his gun no longer pointed at Ed Morin.

Like a pouncing tiger, Ed charged Gerlock, his right hand blurring down on Gerlock's gun arm with a judo chop which snapped bone and sent the Colt .45 skittering off into the water.

Another down-chopping judo blow to the back of the skull, and Kurt Gerlock was knocked senseless. Tommy saw the outlaw's body roll aside as limp as a sack of bones; he saw Ed Morin's lips moving in a victory shout even before his voice reached their ears in the radar shack:

"It's all over, boys! I'll be over to get you in the *Goose* as soon as Cap'n Tucker locks this goon in the galley pantry!"

The *Triton IV*'s twin screws stopped roiling the waters of Cuyler Harbor as Captain Tucker cut his engines; the trapped barge stopped straining to override the hidden obstruction that blocked its exit from the shallow channel of the Devil's Jaw. Only a tugboat could remove the RUM tractor and tow the barge away, and until the harbor was cleared, the Navy would be doing no missile practice on lonely San Miguel.

Inside the radar hut, Tommy felt his back being pounded and his eardrums assaulted by friends in a frenzy of happy thanksgiving, now that danger was behind them.

"We owe you our lives, Tommy, every one of us," Sheriff Ross

Jackson kept saying over and over. "How you were ever able to operate that remote-controlled machine without practice I'll never be able to understand."

Dr. Bonilla expressed it as well as anyone: "Tomás said it was our DX QSO that put us all in this predicament. I say it was his ham radio skill that made him able to operate the tractor and save us all."

Spud Kleveland had his reporter's notebook out again, remembering that he had on-the-spot impressions to record during the time it took Ed Morin to unlock their prison.

"Tommy," Spud said in his best cub-reporter manner, "what thoughts are running through your head right now? What does a hero think about when he's just saved a batch of lives?"

K6ATX scratched his head self-consciously.

"I was just thinking," he said, "how nice it'll be to celebrate my eighteenth birthday tomorrow with my folks. Just think, all this week Dad and Mom have thought I was risking my neck mountain climbing in Washington—when all along I've been safe and sound in California—practically in my own back yard."

Mr. Kleveland commented drily, "I might take exception to that 'safe and sound' stuff, Tommy, but skip it. I can edit Spud's story when it hits the copy desk tomorrow."

Spud was disappointed with the quotation Tommy had given him; it didn't sound very heroic or melodramatic.

"One more thing," Spud said. "I want help on thinking up a headline to fit a real ding-dong doozie-roo of a story. Something that will combine electronics and pirates—you know."

The others were too busy watching Ed land the *Galloping Goose* on the nearby beach to answer Spud, so Tommy obliged.

"A pirate-sounding headline?" K6ATX grinned. "How about this: *'Yo-ho-ho and a throttle of RUM'*?"

▪▪▪ ▬ ▪ ▬

AUTHOR'S NOTE

DX Brings Danger is the third ham radio adventure novel starring Tommy Rockford, K6ATX (the first two were *SOS at Midnight* and *CQ Ghost Ship!*), and if the readers of this book are anything like the readers of the first two, you may find yourself with a hankering to become a radio ham yourself.

Well, you'll never regret it! There are about a half million hams in the United States alone, and a new ham puts his station on the air about once every ten minutes.

How do you go about it? It's easy. If you're ten or twelve years old, a good way to start is to become an SWL, or short-wave listener. Be sure the receiver you buy has a "BFO" or beat-frequency oscillator in the circuit, however; otherwise you can't listen to Morse code, which is the most fun of all—and you have to know the code before you can get a ham license.

After a few weeks of listening to radio amateurs all around the world ragchewing via short waves, you'll get an urge to join the fun. At this point, contact your local radio club for information—they may conduct classes in code and radio theory. If not, or if you live on a farm or other isolated spot, drop a postcard to the American Radio Relay League, Newington, Connecticut 06111, requesting their free packet of beginner information.

Your parents may ask, "How expensive is amateur radio?"

The answer to that is, "As expensive as you want to make it."

You can build your own eighty-meter CW (code) transmitter, good for a one-thousand-mile range, out of junk parts. It is best to spend the bulk of your radio budget for a good communications receiver, for later, if you find that hamming isn't your cup of tea, you can always use that piece of gear.

174

You can buy ham gear in kit form and save a lot of money—besides having the fun of putting together a piece of electronic equipment that works.

By shopping for second-hand gear, you should be able to get on the air with a Novice Class station for under $200. From then on the sky is the limit.

Good luck and vy 73,
WALKER A. TOMPKINS, K6ATX

ABOUT THE AUTHOR

If you have seen the credit line "story by Walker A. Tompkins" flash on your TV screen following some episode of *Death Valley Days*, *Lone Ranger*, *Cheyenne* or *Cisco Kid*, you may wonder if he is the same author who wrote DX BRINGS DANGER and its predecessors starring radio ham Tommy Rockford (SOS AT MIDNIGHT and CQ GHOST SHIP!). He is. And in this book Mr. Tompkins has brought television into the plot of a ham radio adventure. The "RUM" tractor, by the way, really exists.

San Miguel Island, where much of the action of DX BRINGS DANGER takes place, is about thirty miles off the coast of Southern California where Mr. Tompkins lives, at Santa Barbara.

In his home town, Mr. Tompkins is best known for his twice-daily history talks on Radio Station KBLS and his numerous books on regional history and biography. He has been a licensed radio ham since 1952, when he first heard of the Novice Class license, passed the examination and was assigned K6ATX as a station call. He is a former president of the Santa Barbara Amateur Radio Club and has written articles about the hobby for the American Radio Relay League, *National Geographic Magazine*, *CQ*, *Parents' Magazine* and *Popular Electronics*.

During his writing career Mr. Tompkins has traveled all over the world, Egypt and Japan being his favorite spots, with the South Seas and Italy as runners-up. During World War II he served for three years as a war correspondent in Europe.

Readers of DX BRINGS DANGER may be interested to know that the search for Cabrillo's lost grave on San Miguel Island is still going on—whenever the US Navy permits a landing.

DX BRINGS
DANGER
PROOF OF
PURCHASE

ARRL MEMBERS

This proof of purchase may be used as a $0.50 credit on your next ARRL purchase or renewal 1 credit per member. Validate by entering your membership number — the first 7 digits on your *QST* label — below: